GOOD DOG

SCHOLASTIC INC.

This book was originally published in hardcover by Scholastic Press in 2018

ISBN 978-1-338-05389-0

10 9 8 7 6 5 4 3 2   18 19 20 21 22

Printed in the U.S.A.   40
First printing 2018

Book design by Nina Goffi

To all the good dogs I've been lucky to know.
Maggie, Jake, Corona, Annie, Tommy, Sophie, and Odie:
This one's for you.

CHAPTER ONE

Brodie didn't remember the exact moment that he died. But he did remember the exact moment that he woke up afterward.

When he woke up, he was already running.

The grass was wet under his paws. It felt cool and clean and new. Like morning.

The muscles in his legs flexed and stretched and bounded. They were strong. They were *fast*.

His tongue flopped as he gulped mouthfuls of sweet air.

He barked, a free and wild bark, up at the blue skies above him. It was a *yes* bark, a *hooray* bark.

He wasn't being chased. He wasn't afraid. Or tired. Or hungry. Or hurting.

He was . . . *happy*.

The word floated into his head and stayed there.

Happy.

It was his very first word. Just like that, he had it, in his head, and he *knew* it. He knew what it meant. He knew what it felt like. The word sizzled in his head like a piece of hot-from-the-pan salty bacon in his mouth.

Happy.

His tail was all wag.

Tail. That word was next. Then, *wag*. And right after it: *running*.

He barked again, a *happy* bark, loud and joyful.

And then another bark answered him.

He turned his head and saw a dog, running beside him. She was long and lean, with short brown fur the color of good wet mud. *Dog.* That was an important word, he knew. It was *him.* He was *dog.* And then: *mud.* Yes. That was a truly wonderful word. *Mud!* That word made him so happy that he barked again, a high playful *yip.* He felt the word *mud* in his head, sloppy and slurpy and squishy, and he barked out how much he liked that word.

The other dog barked back.

She was matching him stride for stride, her ears bouncing, her eyes shining. Everything he saw put new words into his head: *Eyes. Ears. Shining.*

She stretched out her long legs and got her nose just ahead of Brodie's.

Play! The word shouted itself into his understanding.

He pushed his muscles harder and added length to his strides, as he added two words to his growing collection: *race* and *faster!*

Brodie turned his eyes forward and the world filled in around him. When he'd woken, it had been only the grass under his paws and the sky above his head and then *her.* But now, like a fog was blowing away, he saw a great green field stretching down before him to a river, blue and sparkling. Here and there were clumps of trees and bushes. And all around him and in front of him and beside him were *dogs.* Dogs running. Dogs jumping. Dogs chasing and barking.

Dogs rolling in that sweet soft grass. Dogs splashing in the river.

They were all sizes. All colors.

And all the tails were wagging. And not a single lip was pulled up in a snarl.

Happy.

All those dogs, each one of those wonderful running splashing playing barking dogs, were *happy*.

Brodie and the brown dog raced down a gentle slope and toward the river, taking turns being first. His charging legs ate at the ground with great galloping bites. His muscles were a celebration as they churned. *Running!*

They thundered down the hill and splashed through the muddy shallows of the river, romping and kicking up the water between them.

And as they ran, more and more words rose up and took root in Brodie's mind. *Tree, bush, teeth, leaf, after, before, rocks, sunshine, claw, water, follow, splash, sand. Friend.*

They ran fast, and faster, and fastest, and his legs never got tired. His lungs sucked at the air but never came up short of breath.

Finally satisfied, they flopped down together on the edge of the river, half in the cool flowing water and half on the grass of the shore.

Brodie looked down at the smooth blue water and saw a dog looking back up at him. *Reflection*, his mind whispered. *You*. He saw short white fur, with a dark black spot around one eye. He saw one ear that perked up, another that flopped forward. A wet, black nose. *Me*, he thought.

The brown dog lapped at the water, drinking in big, gulping swallows, then looked up at him with smiling eyes and a dripping snout.

"You're new, aren't you?" she asked.

Brodie cocked his head. His tail stopped wagging. Her question startled him.

It wasn't the words. Yes, they were new, but as soon as she asked them they were there, in his head, and he knew them.

No. It was her voice. It didn't come from her mouth. She didn't bark her words, or growl them.

The words—and her voice—were just there, in his head.

"Oh, you *are* new!" she said in her soundless voice that he could nevertheless hear. "You're still getting your words and everything!"

For the first time since waking, Brodie felt something less than happy.

He felt confused. Scared, even.

His tail slowed, then drooped.

"Oh, don't worry," she said, straightening up. "Really. It's all good." She stepped forward and nudged her chin under his nose, licked at the corners of Brodie's mouth. She was telling the truth.

She was a good dog. Believe me, she was.

"Here," she said. "Start with this: What's your name?"

Name, Brodie thought. He rolled the word around in his head like a toy with a squeak hidden inside. *My name is me*, he thought. *It is what I'm . . . called.*

He shook his head. He searched through the clouds in his heart, looking, trying to remember.

But Brodie? He couldn't remember anything. Not one thing. A whimper grew in his throat.

Then, out of nowhere, it came to him. Brodie's name floated right into his mind and settled there like a drifting feather. Almost like an angel put it there.

It was a name he had never said, because he had never talked. But it was a name that he'd heard a hundred, a thousand, a million times. All at once he could hear it. He could hear it being called, and laughed, and whispered. He could hear it being shouted.

"Brodie," he said, and his answer did not come up from his throat or out through his mouth but, somehow, just from his thoughts to hers. Just like her words had come to him.

"Brodie," she said, and wagged her tail harder. "Hi, Brodie. My name is Sasha."

"Sasha," Brodie said to her, and then he barked with his mouth and it was another happy bark.

He slurped at the water with a thirsty tongue, scattering his reflection into ripples. The water was sweet, and pure, and cold enough to give his mouth happy shivers. And another word appeared to him: *perfect*.

"It's great, isn't it?" Sasha said.

"What, the water?"

She showed her teeth, happy, and raised her nose to sniff at the sunshine and the air.

"All of it."

He looked around. At the sun-sparkled water. The green grass. At all those dogs, all those wagging tails.

"Yes," he answered. But he kept looking. As far as he could see. He looked left and he looked right. He turned his head to look at all that bright world around him.

Brodie was looking for something. Something that was . . . missing. He didn't know what it was. But he knew without a doubt that it wasn't there.

Because Brodie? He had one of those hearts that doesn't forget for long.

"But," he started to say, but he had no words to finish. He cocked his head, confused.

"Yes," Sasha said, and her voice was soft, serious, understanding. "I know. You're trying to remember. And you will," she added, reaching to tap at Brodie's paw with her own. "Don't worry. You'll remember."

"Remember what?" he asked her.

"Before, Brodie. You'll remember Before here. You'll remember . . . your life."

Life. The word rang in his head and hung there. There were layers to that word, threads that ran through it, light that sparkled within it. And shadows around all its edges. It was a heavy, warm, humming word.

"My life," he repeated. "My life Before. Before I . . ." He closed his eyes, his mind chasing at the words and understanding that he couldn't quite grip, like a ball rolling always just out of reach of his teeth.

"Before you . . . *died*," Sasha said, her voice softer than puppy fur. "Before you died *there*, and came here." She wiggled closer to him, so that their paws were touching. "You're dead, Brodie."

Dead.

Dead. He knew it. Pictures flashed in his mind.

A squirrel, still and stiff, its eyes dull and open, lying in brown leaves.

A bird, its body broken, wings crooked and crushed.

A cat on the side of the road, mouth open but silent, its neck twisted.

Dead. Brodie knew *dead*.

His breath came fast. His ears went down flat. He whined, high and begging.

Sasha scooted even closer, nuzzling at his neck.

"But it's okay, Brodie. Really, it is. Because dying there just means being alive here, and here is *wonderful*."

"There? Dying *there*?"

"Yes. Don't you remember? Don't you remember the world, the world with night and hunger and people? Don't you remember *people*, Brodie?"

People.

He did remember.

Two-legged, tall, the bringers of food. Fingers scratching

behind ears. Petting and praising and scolding. Faces and hands and shoes and smiles and mouths making sounds, sounds that Brodie now knew were *words.*

People.

Remembering them made his stomach twist and his tail wag at the same time. *People.* People were good. People were bad. People were terrible. People were wonderful. He remembered all those things at once, and they were all true.

Flashes of memory, dim and blurry and dark and confused, blinked and disappeared in his mind. Voices. Smells.

Brodie jumped to his feet. He turned in a circle. He whined and scratched at the ground, took a few steps, turned and came back.

"It's all right, Brodie," Sasha said, standing up and pressing her shoulder against his. "You can remember later. There is nothing to be afraid of. Not ever again. Let's run. Let's play. Come on." She turned and trotted off, looking back over her shoulder for him to follow.

But Brodie didn't follow her, and she came back to where he stood.

He was almost, almost, almost remembering. But the remembering didn't feel all right. It didn't feel easy. There were shadows. And shouts. And a feeling of leaving. Of leaving when he shouldn't have, leaving when he didn't want to.

And then, in pieces and bits and little broken half pictures, some memories broke through.

A house, with long grass and a falling-down fence and a car in the driveway that never moved.

A park. A park with swings that people rode on, back and forth, up and down. And metal slides they whooshed down with laughing voices. A park with tables you could hide under to be safe from monsters.

A room with closed curtains and a couch with too many smells and a blaring bright box full of pictures that moved and sounds that made no sense, always blaring, night and day.

And in all those splintered half memories, there was *happy* and there was *sad* and there was *scared*, all tangled and tied up together. But it was all so murky.

And right behind it all, lurking just beyond where he could see, was one growling monster of a memory. He could feel it. It had teeth and claws and a shadow, and Brodie whined just from feeling it. But he couldn't see it.

"Brodie?"

He closed his eyes, reaching and searching for more memories of that other world, something clear and strong, something to explain the pain in his chest and the desperate urgency that made the hair on his neck stand straight, like a fight was coming and he was in it.

It was important. Somehow, deeply, Brodie knew that. Remembering it was absolutely the most important thing in any world. There was something he *needed* to remember more than he'd ever needed anything.

And then he did.

A new word came to him.

It flashed like fire into his thoughts. Into his soul. And his heart went still.

Boy.

Boy.

And then: *my* boy.

And with the words came the memory of a face. A face he could see smiling, and crying, and angry, and sleeping, and flinching, and pulling in close to kiss his own. And then a voice. A voice laughing, and singing, and whispering, and shouting. And then a smell, a smell of skin and sweat and clothes and soap and food and boyness that all added up to one beautiful, perfect boy. *My boy.* And Brodie's heart soared and it filled and it emptied and it exploded and it sang and it ached and bled and pounded and stopped, all at once.

My boy.

Something tickled at the very edges of his thoughts. An echo of a memory, of something he did with that boy that he loved. A going away, and a coming back. Away. And Back. Those words came to Brodie, but also their *meaning*, their *feeling*.

Brodie held on to the words strong, not letting go, chasing the memory behind them. And then, like a splash of water, the memory was there. It flooded his mind, soaked his soul in feeling.

Sunlight. But fading, sideways, end-of-the-day sunlight. He was running, paws drumming on dirt and grass. Away from his boy. And then Back. Away. And Back.

The boy was throwing something. Round, yellow, fuzzy. Ball. *It was slobbery and warm from his mouth, stained and gritty from the muddy grass. He sprinted after it and snatched it up, again and again and again, his lungs heaving and his legs burning but his heart happy, happy, happy.*

He dropped the ball at the boy's feet for the hundredth time, his tongue hanging out through his exhausted panting. The boy was smiling his wide smile that Brodie knew, and Brodie loved.

At the edge of the park, a streetlight buzzed on.

The boy looked up and eyed the darkening skies, the coming night. His smile faltered. A thin line of worry knotted his brow.

"It's time to go home, Brodie," he said. He looked again at the growing darkness, then back over his shoulder. Back toward the home they would return to. He swallowed, and Brodie saw his Adam's apple bob.

He looked back to Brodie and propped a smile up onto his face. It wasn't as wide as before, as easy. As real.

"Nah," he said, shaking his head. "Let's do a few more throws, okay, Brodie?" Brodie had wagged his agreement. The boy had picked up the ball. He'd looked over his shoulder one more time, then back to Brodie. That smaller smile, sad and serious, was still on his face. That smile? That smile was just for Brodie. "Just a little longer, boy."

And he'd reared back and thrown the ball, a mighty arcing throw. And Brodie had rocketed after it.

And his boy, that sad and serious boy standing in the shadows, had cheered him on.

"Go, Brodie, go! Go, Brodie! Go!"

Brodie's legs had churned as fast as he could make them. He was pure determination. He was love with legs. He would chase that ball his boy had thrown. He would catch it. And he would bring it back, through any shadows and through all darkness, to his boy.

Brodie had flown.

Away. And Back.

Brodie stood, tingling and breathless with the memory of his boy, of being with his boy.

But now? Now Brodie was Away from his boy. Far away. The distance and the separation pulled at him like a tugged leash, calling him back.

And when Brodie remembered him, when he remembered his boy, that darker monster of a memory growled louder and grew bigger and the coldness of its shadows made all his body shiver.

Danger. The word stabbed into him. Then: *need*. And then: *help*.

Across that gulf between whatever world he was in and that other world that he could barely remember, he could taste and smell and feel the words *boy* and *need* and *help* and *danger.*

He opened his eyes. His tail was still. But his body shook.

Because his heart was telling him exactly what he needed to do.

And Brodie? Brodie was one of those wonderful souls who, when his heart told him to do something, he did it. Yes, he was.

Brodie looked at Sasha and he said the desperate, crazy, urgent truth that quivered alive in his hero's heart.

"I have to go back."

CHAPTER TWO

"What do you mean, go back?" Sasha's voice was low and serious.

"I need to go back. To the world with . . . people." *To the world with my boy,* he thought, but he didn't say it.

Sasha blew a breath out through her nose.

"You can't go back, Brodie. And . . . why would you even want to?"

Brodie thought of the boy's face, *his* boy's face, and of that monstrous memory, and of the shapeless shadowy feeling of danger. He poked at that feeling in his head, but it didn't get any clearer.

"I . . . I don't know. I just know that I need to."

He paced, turning and looking around, looking for . . . for . . . for what? Words rose in his mind: *Door. Gate. Stairs.*

But Brodie's eyes found nothing but grass and water and trees and romping dogs.

He whined a miserable whine high in his throat. He strained his eyes into the distance. *This place can't go on forever,* he thought. *There must be an end to it somewhere.*

He picked a direction and started jogging, along the river.

"Brodie?" Sasha called after him. "Hey, wait up!"

She ran alongside him, her long legs easily keeping up with his.

"Where are you going?"

"Back," he said, not slowing down. "I'm leaving here and going back."

"It doesn't work like that, Brodie."

"How do you know? Have you ever tried?"

"Well, no. But I know you're wasting your time."

"Maybe. But I have to try."

"Stop, Brodie. Listen to me." He knew she was trying to help, but he didn't slow down. "Stop!"

Sasha stopped running and Brodie heard her panting breath fade as he kept going.

"Brodie!"

Her voice got sharper, louder. "Wait!" she called out. "Do you really want to find a way out of here?"

He stopped, then turned and faced her. She stood, her tail down and her ears up, looking at him.

"Yeah, Sasha. I need to."

She looked away, licked at her nose, then looked back at him.

"Okay. Then come with me. You need to talk to Tuck."

"Who's Tuck?" Brodie asked as he followed Sasha up the hill, away from the river.

"He's one of us," she answered. "He's been here longer than anyone else. If anyone knows how to go back, it'll be him. He's usually running around up here by the pond."

Pond. Once she said the word, he knew it. He could

picture the water. And then it was there in front of them, sparkling in the sunlight. Dogs ran around it, and lazed in the shade of a few trees, and splashed in the shallows or swam deeper, their heads bobbing across the surface.

Sasha scanned the romping dogs.

"Ah, there he is. Running, of course." She pointed with her chin. "That big guy. The fast one."

The fast one. That's all she needed to say. There were dogs walking around the pond and dogs jogging around the pond and even some dogs running around the pond . . . but there was only one dog straight-up *racing* around the pond. His tongue was flapping and his ears were down tight to his head and that dog was a thundering black blur.

He was on the far side of the pond but coming fast, his muscular body stretched long with his strides. Sasha jogged forward to get in his path and as he careened toward her she barked and hollered, "Hey, Tuck! Tuck, hold up a sec!"

Tuck's ears perked up and he straightened his front legs, digging his paws into the grass and sliding to a wild, skidding stop. He had a thick square snout and a white blaze on his chest. Other than that, he was pure shiny black from his wet nose to his short, stubby tail. And that tail was wagging almost as fast as the rest of him had been running.

That Tuck. He was all run, all wag, all toothy smile. He had the hard muscles of a warrior, but the sloppy smile of a puppy. Tuck? Well, he was quite a dog.

"Hey there, Sasha," he said, his voice ringing in Brodie's head just like Sasha's did. He was breathing fast and happy but he wasn't out of breath, and he danced from foot to foot, like he couldn't wait to be running again.

"Hiya, Tuck."

The black dog looked over at Brodie. "Who's your friend?"

"This is Brodie. He's new. Like, *brand*-new."

Tuck's mouth stretched into an even bigger smile and his tail wagged double time.

"Really? Welcome, buddy!" He stepped forward, sniffing hello. "Say, what breed are you?"

"Breed?"

"Yeah, you know, like what'd your people call you? Lemme guess . . . border collie? You definitely got some border collie in ya. But not purebred, right? Nah. No offense. You're kinda small. Fur's too short, too. Maybe a little Jack Russell terrier in there? Am I close?"

Brodie couldn't keep up with Tuck's questions. They were too fast, with too many new words, and delivered without a breath. Tuck circled him as he talked, all friendly sniffs and bright eyes and wagging tail.

"What?" Brodie finally managed to say. "Um . . . I don't know?"

"Ah, well, it'll come to you. Me, I'm purebred American Staffordshire terrier. Papers and everything. That's a mouthful, though, so you can just call me a pit bull. It's basically the same thing. I was supposed to be a show dog, but I, uh, had trouble with the standing still part. And the being quiet part. And with almost all of it, really."

Tuck stopped his circling long enough to scratch his claws into the grass a few times and shake his rump in the air.

"Hey! You like running?"

"Um, sure, I guess . . ."

"You *guess*? What's not to love? Running is my absolute most *favorite* thing in the whole world. How 'bout you? If it's not running, what *is* your favorite thing in the world?"

Brodie stared at the grinning black blur of energy before him.

"I don't know," he answered. It was the truth.

"Huh. Well, it'll come to you. You sure it's not running? 'Cause you look fast. Are you fast? Wanna run, buddy?"

"Uh, thanks," Brodie answered, talking fast to get his words in between Tuck's nonstop chatter. "But . . . I need to ask you about something." He looked at Sasha and she wagged her tail, urging him on. "I . . . I don't want to stay here."

Tuck spun in a quick circle where he was standing.

"All *right*! Wanna head down to the river? I'll race ya!"

His eyes sparkled and his legs quivered, ready for the chase.

"No. I mean, I don't want to stay *here*. At all. I don't wanna be in this whole place."

Tuck's tail slowed, and he looked at Brodie out of one eye. When he spoke again his voice was still mostly friendly, but some of his cheerfulness was gone.

"Yeah? All right. Sorry to hear that, but . . . if you're ready to move on, go for it."

Before Brodie could ask what he meant, Sasha cut in.

"No, Tuck. Brodie doesn't want to move on. He wants to go *back*."

Tuck's mouth pulled closed.

"Go back?" he asked quietly. "Like, *back*, back? To Before?"

"Yeah," Brodie said. "I *need* to. Right away."

Tuck looked intently into Brodie's eyes for a long moment.

"Tell him, Tuck," Sasha said. "Tell him he can't—"

"I *can*," Brodie interrupted. "You just said I can move on if I'm ready. Well, I'm ready."

Tuck shook his head.

"You don't get it. Moving on is not going back. Moving on is going *forward*. What you're talking about, that's . . . that's a whole different thing."

"But . . . but . . . ," Brodie stammered, holding on to the wisp of the memory of his boy.

Tuck stepped in close.

"I know. You're new. It's confusing at first. Let's go for a walk. Let me show you how it works around here. All right?"

Brodie looked at Tuck, then down at the ground. An ache grew in his chest, a sharp ache that came from those shapeless memories, that shadowy feeling of danger, that vague remembering of his boy, and the feeling that somehow, somewhere, that boy needed him.

Brodie took a breath in, then blew it out. He looked back up at Tuck.

"Yeah," he said. "Okay."

The three of them set off, walking back down through the trees toward the open fields by the river. Even Tuck's walk was fast, and Brodie had to jog from time to time to keep up. As they walked, Tuck talked.

"So, you've figured out the basics already. We all had lives, back Before. In that other world, with people and stuff. And then, one way or another, we died. You remember how you died yet?"

"Uh, no."

"Okay. Don't worry about it. You will. Anyway, we died. And we ended up here. And here is *not* a bad place to be. We've got everything we need. Everything we could ever want."

Brodie looked around at the grass, the water, the dogs playing chase and basking in the sunlight.

"So . . . this is it? We just . . . stay here?"

"Nah. This ain't a Forever place. We stay here a while. We get words, we get some . . . understanding. Piece by piece we remember our lives. And then . . . we're ready to move on."

"To where?"

Tuck paused.

"We don't know. But . . . it's a good place. Like, the *best* place."

"How do you know that?"

"It's just a feeling. You'll see."

They walked on a bit in silence, the grass soft beneath their paws.

"Here, wait. Hold on," Tuck whispered suddenly, and they all stopped. His body was stiff, and Brodie looked where he was looking.

He didn't see anything strange. In the distance, a group of dogs was wrestling in a mud puddle. A little closer, a tiny long-haired dog sat, looking down the slope to the river.

"What?" Brodie asked.

"That terrier," Tuck said, pointing with his nose at the little furry dog. "This is how it goes. I've seen it a million times. He's about to do it." Tuck sat, settling down on his haunches, and Sasha and Brodie did the same.

"Do what?" Brodie asked, matching Tuck's low whisper.

"Move on," Sasha answered, and her voice was shaking with excitement.

Brodie looked over at her, saw her eyes shining and her body quivering, and then he looked back at the little dog.

He was just sitting, looking out at that perfect world. He looked quiet. Calm. Even from a distance, Brodie could see his chest rise as he took a deep breath, held it, then released it.

Then, syrup-slow and out of nowhere, it happened.

There was something different about him. Brodie hadn't looked away, but all at once there was a *difference*. He blinked and then he saw it. There was a glow. A golden glow around him, shimmering off his brown coat.

Then, reaching from the clouds above, a long beam of matching golden light stretched down. Not with a flash, but with a warm seep, like the sun rising. But it was a sunrise just for him.

His little tail began to wag.

When the light from the sky reached the glow around the dog, he rose up. His body left the ground and the glow brightened. All around him floated little golden balls of light, like fireflies. They circled him in a gentle dance.

As he lifted toward the sky, as the glowing grew and the twinkling lights swirled, the dog's body began to fade. It didn't fade into nothingness, though . . . it faded into light. His body glowed and faded and merged with the light, rising and growing brighter at the same time that it disappeared.

And then, just like that, it was over.

The golden light was gone. The swirling stars were no more. There was just green grass and blue sky. But the little dog was gone.

Brodie sat, breathless. His tail had gone past wagging to stillness.

It was something. It really was. Something you see once and are never the same again after.

"That's it," Tuck said, his voice soft. "That's moving on. We call it 'Forevering.'"

"Forevering?"

"Yeah. Because that world we came from, that was just for a while. And this one here is for even shorter. But the next place? That's the Forever place."

Tuck blew out a breath, then his tail thumped on the grass behind them.

"So, there you go," he said briskly. "That's Forevering. And that, buddy, is what you should be shooting for."

He bent down to scratch at his ear with a hind paw, but he paused when his eyes caught Sasha. She was still looking at the spot where the little dog had been. Her eyes were still shining.

"You all right there, Sasha?" Tuck asked.

"What? Yeah," she said, shaking her head. She wagged her tail and panted cheerfully. Tuck sat stone-still, looking at her.

"What?" she asked again.

"Nothing," he said. But there was something that sounded a little like sadness in his voice.

Because Tuck? He was crazy and he was fast and he was wild, but he was also wise in a lot of ways. And looking at Sasha right then, he *knew.* But he just finished his scratching and shook his ears out.

"So . . . when does it happen?" Brodie asked. "Like . . . when are we ready?"

"It depends," Tuck said. "Some dogs run around, splash in the river, and then go straight to Forevering. For others, it takes a little longer. But everyone Forevers eventually."

Without warning, he flopped over onto his back, kicking his legs and twisting to scratch his back in the grass.

"Well," Sasha said. "Except for you."

"Me?" Tuck said, still rolling. "Eh. I ain't in no rush."

"How long have you been here?" Brodie asked.

"Who knows?" Tuck stopped rolling and jumped up, then spun in a quick circle. They'd clearly been standing still too long for Tuck. "Longer than anyone else. But not long enough, I guess. I like it here. I'll Forever someday. That's how it works, buddy. There's no use fighting it."

All the peace that Brodie had felt after watching the little dog faded.

No use fighting.

It came back in flashes: *His boy's face. Angry voices. Darkness. Fear. The terrible feeling of leaving. The taste of danger in his mouth.*

"No," Brodie said. "I . . . I . . . have to go back."

Sasha nuzzled at his ear.

"Listen to him, Brodie. You can't go back." She spoke softly, gently. "It's impossible."

"Well, I said there was no use," Tuck interrupted, scratching at a rock stuck in the dirt at his feet. "I didn't say it was impossible."

"What?" Brodie said. His heart sparked with sudden hope. "How?"

"There *is* a way," Tuck went on, stopping his playing long enough to look up at Brodie. "But you don't want to do it, buddy. Trust me. Forget about going back."

"I can't," Brodie said. There was a growl in his voice. "I have to go back. If there's a way, show it to me. Please."

"Why?" Tuck asked, going to work on the rock again, bending down to gnaw at it with his teeth. "What's so important? Why do you need to go back?"

"Because. Because I . . ."

Brodie gritted his teeth hard, like he was gripping something that his very life depended on. And he tried, with everything in him, to remember. He closed his eyes.

He thought of his boy. Of his face, his voice, his smell.

A wisp of a memory came to him. Laughter. Wagging. Sunlight. Brodie grabbed the threads of the memory, held them tight with his teeth, pulled them in. And then he had it.

It was him and his boy, chasing each other through piles of thick squishy coldness. A word came with the memory: snow. *They were at a park, the same park he'd had blurry visions of earlier, and their breath puffed in front of their faces in little white clouds. The slides were empty; the swings were still and draped with snow. It was just him and his boy and the snow, and the sky was a cloudless powdery blue above them. The boy's cheeks were red and his lips were chapped but pulled wide in a smile.*

The boy bent and scooped a handful of snow into a ball and tossed it, calling, "Catch, Brodie!" Brodie snapped at the ball and it exploded, filling his mouth with coldness and wetness and a taste like water but more. He shook the snow out of his eyes and barked for another. His boy laughed, a deep laugh from way down in his belly, and it was the best sound in the whole world. He threw another snowball, and another, and Brodie caught them all, and the boy laughed every time. Brodie was standing, the snow up to his belly, waiting for the next snowball, when a hollered voice from far away stopped his boy in mid-throw. "Aiden!" *it shouted.* "Aiden! Get over here!" *His boy looked in the direction of the voice, and the snowball in his mittened hands fell to the ground. The smile faded from his face.*

"Brodie." Tuck's voice broke the spell.

Brodie blinked, looking around. Tuck was watching him, his head to the side.

"You got one, didn't you?" he asked. "You got a memory."

He opened his eyes. He took a few breaths, trying to calm his heart.

"Yeah. I did," he said, his voice tight with excitement. "There's a boy, Tuck. He's *my* boy. His name—I just remembered his name. It's Aiden. My boy's name is Aiden."

"Your boy, huh?" Tuck's voice was soft.

"Yeah! There was snow and there was laughing. And there was a voice. Another voice." Brodie's wag slowed. "A mean one."

"So, what?" Tuck asked. "So you wanna go back to see your boy one last time? Is that it?"

Brodie blinked. His mind was stuck on that voice, the other one, the angry one. That voice was tied up in the other memory, too . . . the dark, monstrous one with teeth and shadows and fear. The one that lurked and growled just out of reach. He closed his eyes and tried to find it, tried to grab it in his jaws, tried to see it. He found a thread of it and he held on, chasing it down. It was still blurry, still lost in shadows, but he got more of it.

There were sounds. Shouting, slamming. The crash of something breaking. That same furious voice, shouting.

His heart raced, the memory so close he could almost feel it: *His boy's arms around him. The sharp smell of his fear. Aiden was . . .* crying, *that's the word. Warm, salty tears. Shaking breaths. The sound of stomping feet pounding their way . . . Aiden beginning to tremble, holding Brodie tight. Brodie raising his lip in a snarl . . . but his body trembling, too, just like his boy's. "No!" His boy's voice was high, terrified. "Please!" Then, worst of all: "Brodie!"*

Brodie looked at Tuck, and when he spoke, his voice was strong and true and steady.

"No. It's more than that. He's in danger. And he needs me. Take me, Tuck. Now. Please."

There was a moment of weighing, of deciding, with Tuck's brown eyes locked on Brodie.

Brodie didn't know how he knew—maybe it was one of those "understandings" that Tuck talked about—but somehow he knew that Tuck wasn't just thinking about what Brodie had said, or about Brodie's boy. He could see in his eyes that Tuck was thinking about something else, too, something that only had to do with himself. His eyes were clouded with deciding. And then they went clear.

"It's a mistake," he said. "A big one. But fine. I'll take you there." For the first time since Brodie had met him, Tuck's voice was completely serious. Then his mouth opened into a smile, and his tail began to wag. "But if we're going, we're *running*."

CHAPTER THREE

Tuck led them straight up the hill at a dead, reckless run. Away from the river, through the trees, past the pond. The higher they got, the darker the skies became. Blue gave way to gray above them as the friendly clustered trees below gave way to a thicker, grimmer forest. It was a shadow-stained kind of forest, with more branches and fewer leaves. More dirt, and less grass. A shivery, look-over-your-shoulder kind of forest.

But Tuck and Brodie and Sasha? They didn't turn around. Sure, Tuck's ears drooped a bit. And Brodie's tail hung lower. And Sasha did cast looks back the way they'd come, and anxious glances into the gloom that closed in around them. But they didn't turn around.

It wasn't far, where they went, but it felt like a world away from the happy, sun-splashed one they'd left.

And then they were there.

The end.

They followed Tuck around a large boulder and stopped where they were. The gray dirt path they were following went on a few more paces, and then . . . didn't. It ended at the stark edge of a cliff. There was a sheer ledge, a line of stone and dust where the world seemed to end, and beyond it was nothing but blackness, and swirling white fog, and a frigid wind blowing into their faces.

Brodie shivered, and it wasn't just from the cold wind or just from soul-deep fear . . . it was from both.

The whole place—the rocks, the path, the cliff—was blurry and vague. When Brodie looked close at any one spot, he couldn't seem to focus on it . . . his eyes just slid to the side. Like teeth off a bone.

He shifted nervously from paw to paw. Tuck had stopped a few steps in front of him, and Sasha stood by his side.

"Yeah, buddy," Tuck said, his eyes on the inky emptiness at the cliff's edge. "There it is. The way back."

"How do you know?" Brodie whispered, the hair on his neck rising.

"I've seen others go," Tuck said quietly. He looked back at Brodie, and his eyes were sad. His heart was, too. "But they weren't like you, Brodie. They were . . . bad dogs."

Bad dogs. Brodie swallowed back a queasy feeling at the words.

Tuck turned his head to look at the edge, then looked back at Brodie. "Not one of them ever came back, buddy. Not one."

"I don't like this place," Sasha murmured.

"Me, neither," Tuck said. "It's not a good place, Brodie. This isn't what you want to do."

Brodie took a deep breath and walked past him, closer to the rim. His belly was churning and his fur stood on end, but he kept walking, until he was only a few steps away.

It was strange, the darkness that waited beyond the edge. It didn't matter that he got closer, didn't matter that he squinted his eyes and tried to peer down into it. It didn't get any less shadowy. Even only a few steps from the edge, Brodie couldn't see even a paw's length down into it. The darkness was so utter and impenetrable that it seemed like he could have reached out a paw and touched it.

Brodie was shaking. Not just his heart. Not just his paws, or his muscles. Every bit of that dog, inside and out, was shaking.

But Brodie? He took another trembling step forward. Then another. He reached his snout forward. Ready, perhaps, to leap into the darkness.

Because Brodie was a dog with a heart as pure and shining as the color of the sunrise. And there's never been a sunrise that shrank from darkness, no matter how thick or cold it was.

When Brodie's brave paws were mere breaths away from the brink, the angel finally spoke. He had waited as long as he could. He'd wanted to see just how much courage there was in that little black-and-white dog, and how much love.

There was plenty.

"Are you sure?" he asked.

Brodie pulled back from the edge with a jerk. He spun to face the voice.

There was a person sitting on a rock, just a few feet away. He hadn't been there a moment before. Brodie was sure of it. Brodie squinted at him, cocked his head. But just like the rest of that place, he couldn't exactly *see* him. His shape was there, and he could make out a kind face that was younger than an adult's, but not quite a child's. It was more boy than man, though.

"You shouldn't go, Brodie," the boy said, "unless you're really sure. And probably not even then."

Brodie took an uncertain step toward him.

"How do you know my name?"

"Because you're here," the boy answered. "You're here, so I know you. Just like I know Tuck. And you, Sasha."

Sasha's tail wagged, but Tuck stood as still as Brodie did.

"Who . . . what . . ." Brodie struggled with his new words to frame a question. It was a question that the boy sitting on the rock knew well. It was one they always asked him.

"I'm a . . . helper, Brodie. Some would say an 'angel.' That's not quite right, but you can call me that if it's easier. I'm here to help you move on. Or," he added, looking toward the cliff, "to help you stay here."

"I'm not staying here," Brodie said quickly. "And I'm not moving on. I have to go back." His heart was filled with the sound of his boy calling out his name. The angel-who-wasn't-an-angel knew that.

"Come here, Brodie," he said. His voice was gentle; it eased the fur still bristling on Brodie's back.

The angel held out his hand. Brodie hesitated, then looked back at Sasha and Tuck, who stood watching him. They didn't look scared.

Brodie walked forward, into the arms of the angel.

He laid his head in the angel's lap and let him scratch at his ears and pet down the fur on his back. These were hands that had petted dogs before, and knew how to do it right. And every scratch, every pat, and every rub was a memory of people, of how *good* they could be, of how good they could make you feel. Brodie closed his eyes.

"Let me show you, Brodie. You guys, too," the angel said to Sasha and Tuck. "Listen." He knelt down in the dirt, one hand still on Brodie's back while the other pointed, back down beyond the grim forest and toward the riverbank sunshine.

"This place is an in-between place," he said. "A passing-through place. When you came here, you left behind a world of darkness. Look." The angel shifted, turning toward the cliff's edge. Brodie turned with him, staring into that blackness with wide eyes.

The angel swept with his hand at the darkness. The fog churned and thickened. The angel swept his hand again, and a round window opened in the mist before them. Through it sparkled a star-speckled blackness, and then again he swept his hand and a glowing blue orb appeared before them. Brodie knew it. Though he'd never seen it, though he'd never known what it looked like, he knew then that it was the *world*. The world where he'd come from. The world where his boy was.

As he watched, the world zoomed closer. He saw water, he saw land and clouds, and he understood.

He flew with dizzying speed, his paws still standing in dirt but his eyes a world away. Images flashed before him as he raced over the world, images the angel had chosen to show him.

He saw a dog with food-starved ribs pressing through his fur, panting in a pile of garbage. He saw a man raising a stick, his face ugly with anger, as a dog cowered against a wall. He saw a woman and a mutt, shivering together under soggy newspapers as a freezing rain fell and other people walked past without a glance. He saw a limping dog scurrying across a road before a roaring car, too slow; he squeezed his eyes shut as the bumper slammed into the dog's hind legs, spinning the broken body into a gutter. He saw many things. And he understood.

"That world? It can be a dark place. It has violence, and despair, and cruelty, and pain. But there's plenty of good there, too; plenty of light and love and hope. Beauty."

Again the angel swept his hand, and the visions changed. Brodie saw a girl bend down and offer half her sandwich to a stray dog on the sidewalk. He saw a man lifting a dog up a front porch, a dog too old to climb the stairs himself. And he saw the same dog and woman sitting in the rain, but this time he saw the woman reach to pull the newspaper tighter over the dog's shivering shoulder, and the dog lick her grimy hand in thanks. He saw a boy, pale and sick, lying exhausted in a bed—and a dog, sitting patiently by his side, eyes on the boy, never leaving.

"Yeah," the angel said. "Plenty of beauty. And that world is important. It's where we find our goodness, and create our beauty, and prove our courage. But it's all tangled up there. You can't pull the beauty out from the tragedy."

He waved his hand and the flickering parade of moments sped up. It all passed by: pain and patience, kindness and cruelty, mercy and madness. Brodie couldn't look away.

"It's only from up here that you can see it and understand it and find peace. You need . . . the *bigger truth*, Brodie. You need to step out into the light to see the shadows scatter."

Another wave of his hand and, somehow, Brodie saw it all at once. The view zoomed out so that he saw the bright blue world shining in a sea of blackness, but at the same time he could still see all the million moments of beauty and sadness flashing past. And he understood.

The angel dropped his arm and leaned back. The mist swirled again. It filled in the window they'd been looking through. Once again, there was nothing beyond the edge of the dirt except for depthless dark and fog.

"You don't need to go down to find your peace. Your peace will rise to you, if you let it. Everything good rises upward in the end. This place is where your goodness shakes off the last bits of darkness and sadness and shadow, so that you can move on without it. And that's what *you* need to do, Brodie."

Brodie looked up into the angel's warm green eyes.

"What if I can't?"

The angel pursed his lips.

"There are some who think they can't. They get stuck here. Or, worse, they try to go back, like you. But listen, Brodie. If you're stuck here, it's because there's something back there holding you. Something that you can't make peace with or let go. And sometimes, yeah, going back can help souls let go and move on to Forever. But listen. It's almost never. *It's almost never.* Most who go back . . . it just makes them hold on tighter. It makes it even harder to let go. And they stay until . . . until their life is gone. Their soul. And they're stuck there. Not alive, not dead, just . . . shadows. Stuck in the darkness like mud. Ghosts."

Brodie understood, somehow, all that he had said. He could *feel* it, deep in the soul of himself. He could almost taste the truth in the angel's words.

And yet.

Still echoing in his heart was that dark memory, the memory of his boy's fearful face and the gnawing feeling that Aiden needed him and that he had let him down. He shook his head, trying to clear his thoughts.

And Brodie? He *tried* to see through to that bigger truth.

But he couldn't. Because one thing wouldn't budge: the hard tug of his love for that boy. That love was the biggest truth he could ever imagine.

Brodie looked into the blackness. Then he looked back up to the angel.

"I . . . I . . . I have to go back. I'm sorry. I have to see my boy."

The angel's brow furrowed. His mouth tightened. He leaned forward. When he spoke, his voice was still kind, but its softness had been replaced by a hard sort of truth.

"Listen, Brodie. You say you want to see your boy again. I understand. Believe me. I do. But that's why you *have* to stay here. If you go back, you may never see your boy again."

"Why?"

"Because, Brodie. Whatever's gonna happen back there in that world is gonna happen. You're done with that world now. And it's done with you. Someday, your boy will move on, like you did, and be in a place a lot like this one. And then your boy will let go, and be free, and move on to Forever. And you can be there waiting for him, Brodie. And then you can be *with* him again, Brodie. Truly with him. But only if you get there. If you go back now, like you want to, you'll be able to *see* your boy, maybe . . . but you won't be with him, not really. And then you'll be stuck, almost for sure. And you'll lose your soul. And your boy will move on. And you'll never, ever be with him again. If you lose down there, Brodie, you lose everything."

The angel took his hand off Brodie's back. He stood up and stepped to the edge of the darkness. He held his hands up.

"If you want to go, go. Jump. I can't stop you. But if your boy were here, he would tell you not to do this, Brodie. He would beg you to stay here and not do this. Believe me."

The angel sighed. He looked out into the depthless, wind-howled blackness, then back to the dog at his feet.

"So. That's your choice. Do you want to, Brodie? Do you want to go back?"

Brodie's soul was a battleground.

When he thought of that one monstrous memory, of his boy in danger and screaming his name, every part of him wanted to charge forward, to leap off into that blackness and save him. But then he thought of what was at stake. Of what the angel said he'd almost certainly lose: himself. His soul. His boy, forever. Forever.

"I want . . . ," he said. He looked down into the waiting darkness. "I want . . ."

But then the angel hushed him.

"Wait," he whispered. "Shhh." Brodie looked up, then followed the angel's gaze to where Sasha stood.

She'd listened to everything. She'd looked into the blackness. She'd looked back at the sunshine, the river, the green. She'd looked. And she'd listened.

And Sasha? She'd figured it out.

She'd walked a little away from the rest of them, back down the path. Her body was still, her ears up. Her eyes were not on the distant water, or the fog-swirled cliff . . . they were looking up. Up at the clouds, and up at the blue sky. And up at the single beam of golden light stretching down toward her.

Brodie saw what was happening. He took a quick step toward her.

But Tuck stepped forward. He stood in front of Brodie, his shoulder blocking him. But gently.

Because Tuck? He was a good dog. Even when it was hard.

"I knew she was close," he said. "I could see it when we watched the other dog go."

"But . . . but she . . . ," Brodie started to say.

"No, buddy. She's ready. It's a good thing."

He said the words, but it didn't sound to Brodie like he meant them. Not all the way.

"Here she goes," he murmured. And then she did.

It was just like before. The perfect light. The swirling, glowing fireflies. Sasha glittered and rose and shone. And then began to fade. Brodie whined, softly, just to himself.

The last thing he saw before she dissolved into sparkling gold light was a wagging brown tail.

Then the light dimmed. The floating sparkles winked out one by one. And Sasha was gone.

Brodie's heart, already teetering on the tooth's edge of his choice, trembled at the sight.

It was beautiful, the moving on . . . but it was so clearly *forever.* When Brodie watched it, he could feel it: Forevering rang with permanence. Sasha was gone, and she was gone forever.

"Atta girl, Sasha," Tuck said, his voice a hoarse whisper. "Atta girl."

Tuck sighed and his great black head drooped.

The angel moved to stand beside them. He put a hand on each of their backs.

"That," he said. "That's what you should be doing. Saving your soul. Not throwing it away. I know it's hard. But look, Brodie. Look for the bigger truth. Please. *Please.*"

It was the *please* that did it, that broke Brodie's indecision. It was that *please*, added to the foreverness of Sasha's leaving.

Because when that angel-who-wasn't-an-angel said that one word, the memory came back. The dark one, the monstrous one, the one with teeth. It rose up from the cliff's drop behind him and roared into his head.

And this time, there was more to it.

Once again, there was darkness. His boy's arm was tight around him. But this time there were smells. Sharp, acrid smoke. Cigarettes. *The word was there, tied tight to the bitter memories. And another smell, sour and sickening:* beer. *Somewhere, unseen, a television blared its chaotic noise.*

He could hear Aiden's shuddering breaths, feel the fear in his body pressed against him, and even in a memory it broke his heart and raised his fur and bared his teeth. And mixed in the smell of his fear was the smell of mud. It was part of the memory, somehow, but he didn't know how or why.

There was a shout, a beastly roaring shout, and then footsteps coming toward them. A monster loomed, cloaked in shadows. It lurched toward them, huge and awful and deadly. Brodie cowered, his tail tucked between his legs, and pulled his trembling body up closer to his boy's.

A crash and a shatter.

Kicking feet. Swinging fists.

Aiden, crying out: "No!"

Then: "Please!"

Then, again, his boy's voice breaking and cracking: "Please! No! Please!"

And then Brodie was surging, wiggling free, leaping out of his boy's arms. Running away.

Running away.

There was a blur, a mad confusion of fear and pain and shouting and panic. And then, through the chaos, Aiden's voice.

"Brodie!"

His boy. Screaming. Screaming for him. His voice ragged, terrified, crying.

"Brodie!"

Brodie shook, shattered and sickened by the memory.

"Brodie!"

It was Tuck's voice now, worried and sharp.

Brodie shook his head. He looked at Tuck. He was panting like he'd just been running. He realized he was whimpering, high and desperate, and he swallowed to stop it.

His boy. Frightened. In danger. Alone.

Himself, running away.

Away. And not Back.

"Another memory?" Tuck asked.

Brodie didn't answer.

He didn't care about darkness.

He didn't care about shadows, and when or where they mattered.

He didn't care about peace, or good things rising.

He didn't care about bigger truths. And he didn't care about angels.

He cared about his boy.

That's it.

He looked up at the angel.

"I'm going," he said. "I'm going back. Right now."

CHAPTER FOUR

Brodie stepped up to the waiting black edge of the chasm. The angel moved to stand beside him.

"You said you wouldn't stop me."

"I won't." The angel seemed sad to Brodie. Tired, even. He was.

That brave dog paused. He looked up at the angel and swallowed.

"I'm sorry," he said.

The angel shook his head and bent down to scratch Brodie's chin.

"Oh, Brodie. You don't have to be sorry."

Brodie looked into his eyes.

"Do I just . . . jump off into it?"

The angel nodded.

"Yes. But first, you have to pick a place. *The* place. The place you want to go back to."

"Okay. And then . . . I just . . . end up there?"

"Yeah. But, Brodie, you gotta understand. You're not going back as you were. You're going back as you *are*. A spirit. Nothing more. You're going back to a living world . . . but you're going back dead."

Brodie took a deep breath.

"Okay."

He took a few steps closer to the brink. He peered down

into the gusty, fog-swirled darkness. There was no smell. It just felt cold. His whole body shivered.

"Your spirit will still have life for a while, down there," the angel said. "You'll even be able to see the glow of it. But with each moment in that world, it will fade. When your glow is gone, Brodie, you'll be stuck. You'll be *lost*. Forever."

The word *lost* rattled Brodie's heart; he knew it. Dim memories spoke to him, echoes of feelings and fear: running down a street, looking frantically from house to house, person to person, everything being unfamiliar and strange, sniffing at the air and finding no smells he knew, looking around desperately for his boy. *Lost*. His heart trembled.

The angel knelt down beside him.

"Do what you need to do. And then come back. Before it's too late."

Brodie took a steadying breath.

"How do I come back?"

"When you're ready to return, howl at the moon. Day or night, if you look at the sky, the moon will show itself. Howl, and I'll come for you."

"That sounds easy."

The angel smiled, but like most of his smiles for Brodie, there wasn't much happiness in it.

"Yeah," he said. "It sounds easy. But that world . . . it has ways of holding on. It's a tangled place. And it's the good as much as the bad that won't let you go."

He scratched the dog with strong fingers, down through his fur to the skin. It was a good feeling.

Brodie took another step forward.

"Okay. I'm ready."

He wiggled his nose at the blackness waiting for him. He raised a shaky paw and leaned forward.

"Wait!"

Tuck was walking toward him, his body shaking but his eyes steady.

"Brodie, stop."

"No. I have to do this," Brodie told him.

"Yeah," he said, stopping beside him. "I get it." He looked down into the blackness past his paws, then into Brodie's eyes. "But I'm coming with you, buddy."

Tuck looked to the angel. The angel, again, wasn't surprised.

"I've been here too long," Tuck said. His tail was down, and his clouded eyes dropped to the dirt. "I've watched so many go on to Forever. I've seen them show up here, I've seen them get closer and closer to ready, and then I've watched them go. I know what getting closer looks like. I think I even know what it *feels* like, on the inside. And I've been here all this time and I'm not getting any closer." He swallowed, then looked up at the angel. "I feel like I'm getting farther and farther from ready all the time." He cast his eyes toward the emptiness. "Maybe my peace can't be found up here. Maybe I have to find it down there. With Brodie."

"Listen, Tuck," the angel said. "If you go back with Brodie, you'll be going where he goes. To *his* old life. Not yours. You won't have the—"

"I don't wanna go to my life," Tuck said firmly. "I wanna go with him. Maybe if I . . . if I help him find his peace, I'll find mine. And, if not, I can always just howl, right? And you'll come fetch me?"

There was a laugh in Tuck's voice and a little wag to his tail. But Brodie could tell he was afraid. The angel could, too.

"It's dangerous down there, Tuck. Even more dangerous now than when you were alive."

Tuck's wag broadened.

"All the more reason to keep this guy company. Besides, ain't nothing down there that runs faster than I do." He turned his eyes to Brodie. "Whaddya say, Brodie? Can I come with you?"

The thought of having Tuck by his side when he leapt off into that darkness put some wag into his own tail, too.

Because Tuck? He was exactly the kind of dog you wanted by your side, no matter what you were jumping into.

"Yeah," he answered. "You bet you can."

Tuck stepped forward and the two dogs circled each other happily, tails wagging. Their souls were shining, bright and hopeful and pure. But only the angel could see that.

And it only made him sadder. He didn't know if he could stand to watch two souls that pure and good be lost.

"Maybe this'll be fun," Tuck said, bouncing on his paws.

"Sure," Brodie answered, but his heart was still racing in his chest.

"Do you have a place picked out?"

Brodie stopped and stood still, his eyes closed.

He went through his memories. He only had three. The ball. The snow. And the monster.

He replayed the snow memory: Aiden laughing, the blue sky, the cold that was fun and not scary. The park with its slide and its swings and its places to run and hide. It was a place his boy knew. A place his boy went. And, at least on that one day, a happy place.

"Yeah," he said. "I know where we're going."

"All right," Tuck said, and his tail was all wag now. Tuck was a dog who loved to move, and they'd been standing by that cliff edge for way too long. "Then let's go, buddy."

The angel knelt between them. He put a gentle hand on each of their backs.

"You're good dogs," he said, his voice almost a whisper. "Both of you. Remember that. Be good dogs."

The angel stood.

"Okay. Whenever you're ready. The world is waiting."

Brodie took a step toward the rim. Then another. Tuck's shoulder pressed against his. His tail still had a little wag left in it. Brodie's did not. But they walked together toward the darkness, shoulder to shoulder.

And the angel sat and watched Brodie go. He had to. But he was worried. He was so worried that he rubbed his angel's chin with his troubled angel's hand. He worried because he knew the goodness of those two dogs. And he knew the danger of the world they returned to.

Angels can see a lot. They can see the past and they can see the present. They can see the hearts and thoughts and fears of people—and dogs, and cats, and all things that have hearts and thoughts and fears. But one thing that angels cannot see is the future. And the future is an awfully big thing to not be able to see.

So the angel watched Brodie—that brave, determined dog—leave. And he watched Tuck—that loyal, courageous friend—go with him. And the angel worried.

When Brodie stood with his claws up to the very edge, one jump away from plummeting back to earth, he paused.

The blackness stood waiting like an open mouth to swallow him. His soul trembled at the sight, at the thought of jumping off into it. His courage was holding on by the thinnest edges of its teeth.

Aiden, he thought. *Aiden.* He said the name in his head like a prayer. And with the name came a memory. A new one, just when he needed it. Like a gift from an angel.

It was just Aiden and Brodie. Just those two, together in darkness.

The warmth of a bed. A blanket over them both. Pure blackness, except for a thin sliver of silver slipping in between the curtains on a window across the room.

Brodie, pressed tight against Aiden. Feeling his warmth.

Aiden's breaths, shaking and broken. They were the echoes of sobs.

Brodie whimpered. Just a little. He licked softly at Aiden's face. He tasted salty tears. He tried to clean the sadness from his boy's face. He tried.

Aiden's arm was thrown around Brodie's shoulders. He squeezed, pulling him in even closer. He pressed his forehead against Brodie's. Brodie could see Aiden's eyes, just barely make out the shine of them in that glow of window moonlight, looking fiercely into his own.

And then that boy said four words. Four words that had meant nothing to Brodie the dog, but now meant everything to Brodie the soul leaping into darkness.

That boy held Brodie tight and said: "You. Me. Together. Always."

It was a small memory. There wasn't much to it. No story. Few details.

But that memory? It was everything. It was.

Brodie closed his eyes and held his boy's face in his memory. He took a shuddering breath. He remembered that other memory, the dark and deadly one, with the monster coming toward them both. The smell of Aiden's fear. His voice screaming his name.

He didn't know if he could do this. But he knew he could do it for his boy.

It's easier, sometimes, to be brave when you're being brave for someone else.

He pushed the monster away and imagined that park, that sparkling clear park with the *snow* and the *laughing* and all those wonderful words.

"I'm coming, Aiden," he whispered, and those words were not for Tuck or the angel but were just between him and his boy. "I'm coming for you."

Such a good dog.

He closed his mouth and pointed his ears forward.

And then Brodie?

He jumped.

CHAPTER FIVE

A gust of frigid wind sucked the air from Brodie's lungs.

He squeezed his eyes shut tight. Tuck trembled beside him.

There was a squeezing and a rushing and a feeling like falling.

A great coldness closed its fist around him. A coldness that didn't just touch his fur or his skin or even his bones and his heart; it crept into his thoughts, his memories.

His whole self tingled. Then went numb. Then burned.

A feeling of being upside down and then inside out and then spinning around.

And then stillness.

And then: the feeling of something cold and wet under his paws.

And the sound of a car engine, rumbling in the distance.

And the smell of soil and garbage.

He opened his eyes.

He blinked and looked around.

All he saw was darkness.

For a moment he thought that it hadn't worked. That he was stuck, somehow, trapped between the worlds. A whimper shook in his throat.

But then he looked closer, and shapes began to take form.

In the distance, the faint glow of streetlights. A parked car. A great white snowy field. A couple of swings, empty and still.

He looked up. The moon shone faintly, hidden by dark clouds. The clouds, shoved by the wind, parted. Bright white light flooded down for a moment, revealing the benches and slides and picnic tables standing in paw-deep snow. And he could remember each one. Familiarity swept over him, as warm a feeling as petting fingers.

"Where are we?" Tuck asked from behind him.

"We're at the park," he answered, and his tail began to wag. "We're at my boy's park."

He turned to grin at Tuck and stopped short when he saw him.

"Whoa."

Tuck's eyes were locked on him, too, and they were just as wide as Brodie's.

"Yeah," he echoed. "Whoa."

Tuck was *glowing.* A buttery golden light was sparkling off his fur. And swirling all around him were those same floating firefly lights that they'd seen when a dog Forevered.

"Oh, boy," Brodie whispered. "Just like he said. It's your spirit."

Tuck circled him, his tail wagging slow.

"Yep. You, too, buddy."

Brodie looked down and saw the same glow around his own body, the same drifting lights slowly circling him.

And, standing there, looking at the wondrous glow of his own soul for the first time, Brodie remembered the sound of Aiden laughing. He remembered it from the time they'd played in the snow, but from other times, too: an open-mouthed sound, an eye-sparkling sound, a tail-wagging sound. *Laughing.* The sound of a happy heart. Right then, looking at his own golden fur and glittering cloud of lights, Brodie felt like laughing. He didn't know how laughter worked, but he knew then what it felt like.

Because a soul? It's a beautiful thing to have. And it's a terrible thing to lose. But Brodie didn't know that yet.

Tuck's nose was waving in the air, sniffing at the night smells.

"Smell that, Brodie?" he asked.

Brodie sniffed.

"What?"

"*Everything*, buddy. Just everything."

Brodie sniffed again and knew what he meant.

Up there, where they'd come from, there had been only a few smells, and they were all good and clean and pure. Dirt, grass, water, dogs.

But down here, there were so many more. Brodie smelled oil, and wood, and people. He smelled car exhaust and cooking food and cat pee and the overflowing garbage cans at the park's edge. There were a hundred smells, more even, and some were good and some were bad and they were all mixed together and his nose lapped at them like a thirsty tongue lapping at water. It wasn't that it smelled better—up there had definitely smelled *better,* he thought—but it smelled *more.*

"Come on," Tuck said, and his tail was wagging fierce and his eyes were bright. Brodie knew what he was going to say before he even said it. "Let's run, Brodie. *Let's run.*"

Tuck took off and Brodie was right behind him, trying to keep up. They ran through that cloudy-night park, two dogs with their souls shining like the *fireworks* (the word fizzled to life in his brain as he ran) that Brodie suddenly remembered his boy setting off, right there in that park, on a hot summer night.

And as they ran, more remembering came to him. Memories, one after another, rattling into his head.

They ran past a metal slide, gigantic and sloping, and he remembered: *Aiden, standing at the very top of the slide, waving his arms for balance. A smile that came and went and came again to his face as he concentrated on not falling. Himself, nervous and pacing below, whining and circling. "Will you catch me, Brodie? Will you catch me if I fall?" He didn't know the words then, didn't know the meaning of the sounds his boy was making, but now he did. "Yes!" he wanted to bark up at him. "Yes, Aiden! I'll catch you!"*

They loped past a picnic table, ducking to cut the corner close and scoot under the bench, and he remembered: *Him and Aiden, huddled together under the table while a heavy gray rain fell on the world around them. It drummed on the table above them and plopped in puddles around them and filled the air with its smell and its song. He was happy and wagging, loving the mud and the wetness and the being close with Aiden. But then he saw the fear on Aiden's face, saw his paleness and wide eyes. He was looking down at his clothes, hopelessly muddy. "Oh, man," he was saying, over and over again, a tremble in his voice that had stilled Brodie's tail. "I'm gonna be in so much trouble. Oh man oh man oh man." Brodie licked his hand, licked his face, licked his ear. Trying to help. But failing.*

They circled a rusty old merry-go-round, still and silent, and he remembered: *Aiden, lifting him up onto it, pushing him toward the middle, his claws clicking on the scratched-up metal. "Ready?" His voice, already riffled with laughter. Aiden running, gripping the merry-go-round, faster and then faster and then faster, taking it from a rumble to a squeak to a squeal, and then jumping up onto it with Brodie, breathless and laughing. Aiden's arm tight around him as they watched the world spin and blur around them. And Brodie was happy, even though his paws slid and scraped for balance and his stomach somersaulted. Because when he was with Aiden and Aiden was with him, the world could spin as crazy as it wanted and he knew they'd never fall off.*

And then, out of nowhere, a memory that almost made him stumble and stop: *Darkness. Summer heat. Him and Aiden, crouched in the thickest part of the biggest bunch of bushes in the park, under the trees where the park went wild. Hiding. Aiden's arms around him, so tight he could barely breathe. Aiden was sobbing, and choking, and panting. The smell of tears. The taste of blood. His broken voice. "We'll be okay. We'll be okay. We'll be okay. I love you, Brodie. I love you, Brodie. We'll be okay. We'll be okay. We'll be okay. I love you, Brodie." Over and over and over and over. Him being held too tight, for too long, and his muscles wanting so badly to shake free, to break loose, to move. But not doing it. Staying there tight with his boy. Knowing that Aiden needed that. Knowing that Aiden needed him.*

He stopped running. He looked over to the trees, to where that memory lived.

Tuck noticed and stopped, circled back, came up to him slow.

"Brodie?"

Brodie looked at him.

"I need to find him. Now. I need to know he's okay."

Tuck's run-happy wagging slowed, but he stepped up to snuffle encouragingly at Brodie's ear.

"All right. That's what we're here for, right? Lead the way, buddy."

Brodie sniffed at the air, looking for the memory of which way to go. Tuck followed him through the snow to the sidewalk at the park's edge. It was lit here and there with yellow circles of light from streetlights. A car rolled slowly by, its taillights glowing red. Snow was pushed together in dirty piles along the side of the street, but the road itself and the sidewalk were bare. The concrete sparkled with a thin layer of icy frost.

He looked up the street one way, sniffing the air and eyeing the houses. Most had porch lights on, and lit-up windows. Some were decorated with strings of colored lights along their roofs. *Christmas.* The word came into his mind, and with it a scattershot of half memories: the crinkle of paper being ripped, the crisp scent of a pine tree, the excited eyes of a boy he loved.

He looked the other way. It was darker that way. Some of the houses looked empty, lifeless. A few of the lots between the houses were vacant, with weeds and litter poking up through the snow.

"This way," he said, starting toward the darker houses. "He's this way."

They trotted up the sidewalk, their paws making no sound on the icy pavement. Brodie looked at the houses as they passed, searching for something familiar.

"Are we close?" Tuck asked, padding along cheerfully at his side.

"Kind of. I think. Maybe."

"Oh. Good, I guess."

The houses got more and more run-down as they traveled. There were fewer Christmas lights. Some of the fences were falling down, their paint peeling. Dark porches were cluttered with piles of junk. The sound of an angry voice wafted out of a half-open door.

Ahead, a streetlight flickered. A person leaned against the light post, bundled up in a thick coat. A sharp smell hit Brodie's nose. A familiar smell. *Cigarette.* He knew that smell. It was all tied up with Aiden, with the house that he was looking for.

As they got closer to the man, Tuck suddenly picked up

his pace and got to wagging. Brodie looked up and saw why. The smoking man had a dog, tied to a leash, sitting on the sidewalk next to him.

Tuck barked, a friendly hello kind of bark, but the other dog ignored him. He barked again, but the other dog didn't even twitch an ear.

They got to the corner and Tuck ran right up to that other dog, sniffing and wagging his tail, but that dog did *nothing.*

Tuck barked. He growled. He whined.

"Hey!" he shouted.

Nothing.

"What's wrong with this guy?"

"Tuck, I don't think . . ."

But before Brodie could finish, Tuck jumped forward to nudge the dog with his nose.

But Tuck didn't nudge him. He didn't even touch him. His nose went right through the dog like he wasn't even there, and then Tuck stood there with his whole head stuck inside that other dog.

He pulled it out real quick and stumbled away, his tail between his legs.

Finally, the other dog responded. He shook his head like a fly was in his ear and whined and looked around. But he looked right past Tuck and Brodie. Or, really, right *through* them. Brodie saw the dog's eyes look right at him and there was *nothing* there, not a flicker of understanding.

"What just happened?" Tuck asked, backing away, his fur up and his eyes on the dog.

"The angel warned us, Tuck. We're spirits now, remember? He can't see us. Or hear us."

Brodie stepped right up to that dog so close that their noses were a whisker's length apart. He barked. Then he looked up at the man, who was puffing his cigarette and looking at something in his hand (*phone*, his mind said), his face bored and tired. "People can't, either, I guess."

Tuck crept closer, close enough to sniff at the dog.

"Weird," he said. He stretched a paw forward and timidly stuck it into the dog. It passed right through him. Tuck's tail started to wag again. He lunged forward and stuck his head into the dog, then jumped back. Besides another shiver, the other dog didn't move. Tuck's tail wagged harder. He stuck his head farther in and kept it there for a moment, then jerked it out again. "This is crazy!"

Then his tail stopped wagging and his ears went down.

"Wait," he said. "If we can't touch stuff . . . do you think that means we can't eat?" His voice was deadly serious.

"Who cares?"

"Who cares?! Are you kidding? Did you even hear my question?"

"Um . . . we're *dead*, Tuck. Who cares if we can eat?"

Tuck turned an angry circle.

"Come *on*, buddy! Getting the chance to eat again was half the reason I came back in the first place."

"I thought you came back to help me," Brodie pointed out. "And to . . . move on to Forever."

"Oh, yeah, sure," Tuck said quickly, looking away. "That stuff, too. Mostly. But come on, buddy . . . *eating*?"

"Yeah. I know. It's your second favorite thing in the world. But we've got bigger stuff to deal with than your appetite. Let's go."

Brodie started off again and Tuck reluctantly followed, leaving the smoking man and his dog behind as they continued across the street to the next block.

They passed a woman walking the other way and Tuck barked at her and jumped right through her, wagging his tail. He passed through her like she was nothing but a cloud. She kept walking, but pulled her ratty jacket tighter around her shoulders.

"This is *amazing*!" he said, dancing in a circle. "You gotta try it, buddy!"

"Maybe later," Brodie said, not slowing down. "We're getting close. I can feel it."

They came to the end of another block. The streetlight there was broken, leaving the corner in darkness. Brodie looked one way, then the other. The street was quiet. It was all parked cars and closed doors and city-stained snow. The breeze brought a faint parade of smells to his nose.

"This is it!" he said, his tail going to full rump-swinging wag. "This is the street. This is where we . . ." The words stuck in his throat, and he started over. "This is where he lives. Right down there. I'm sure of it."

"Yeah? All right! Let's go find your boy, then, and . . . hey, look at *those* mutts." Brodie looked to where Tuck was looking, up the street in the direction that they'd been walking. A group of dogs, four of them, were lying around on the sidewalk under a streetlight, half a block ahead. "Wanna go stick our heads in 'em?"

"Nah, Tuck, come on. We're so close!"

"All right, all right. No time for fun. Got it, buddy."

He was still standing facing the distant dogs.

"You mutts are lucky!" he shouted in their direction, then barked. One loud, cheerful bark.

And those dogs? Those dogs down there who shouldn't have been able to see them or hear them?

Well, when Tuck barked, something crazy happened.

All their heads, all four of those dogs' heads, snapped up to look.

Brodie didn't know why, but when those dogs turned their heads toward him, his skin went ice-cold and his tail lost any wag that it had.

CHAPTER SIX

The four dogs stood up, one by one. They cocked their heads at Brodie and Tuck.

Then, one by one, their tails started wagging.

There are lots of kinds of tail-wagging. And when those dogs started wagging their tails, Brodie's mouth went dry. It wasn't the nice kind of wagging. Not at all. It was the kind of wag that a tail does when a dog sees a squirrel on the ground, too far from a tree.

"Hey!" Tuck said brightly. He didn't sound near as anxious as Brodie felt. "Did they hear me? Can they see us?" He barked again, a friendly greeting.

The four dogs started trotting down the sidewalk toward Brodie and Tuck.

"I don't like this, Tuck," Brodie said uneasily, backing up. "I don't like the look of them."

"What are you worried about?" he asked, wagging his tail and taking a few happy steps toward them. They were almost upon them.

The dogs were led by a big golden dog, long-haired and burly shouldered. His mouth was open in a sharp-toothed, eager grin.

"Come on, Tuck, let's . . . ," Brodie started to say. But it was too late.

Before they could run, the dogs were there. And before

Brodie knew what was happening, they were circled around them.

"Hey there, fellas," the big one said. His voice was rough and low and crunchy like truck tires through wet gravel. Brodie blinked, looking hard at the dog's eyes, trying to figure out why they were freaking him out. Then he realized: They didn't have any whites. His eyes were all black . . . pure, shiny black, glittering above his bone-white teeth. Brodie looked around. All of their eyes were like that. Whiteless. Cold.

"Hey," Tuck said, turning a nervous circle to see them all. For the first time his voice sounded unsure, and his fur was starting to rise. Brodie's was already up.

"You, uh, a golden retriever, right?" Tuck asked the leader. "You papered?"

The big dog ignored the question. He stepped closer and the others followed.

"Look at all that glow," the leader said, and his tongue slopped at his lips.

"So much glow!" one of the others said, stepping in closer.

"Oh, man, all that sparkly!" another one hissed, sniffing at them and pawing at the ground.

"You must be brand-new, huh?" the big one asked. He stepped in closer, too, tightening the circle. "Like, fresh from the other side, right?"

"Who are you?" Brodie asked, turning his head, trying to keep them all in his sight.

"Don't worry about it, freshy," he answered, his eyes still on the lights floating around Brodie and Tuck. "You can call me Darkly if you wanna call me something, but, uh . . ." He licked his lips and Brodie saw his own soul reflecting in the blackness of the dog's hungry eyes. "I wouldn't worry about that if I was you."

"Okay, but, like, who *are* you? I mean . . . why can you see us?" Tuck asked, more fur now rising on his back.

"Oh, that's easy," Darkly answered. He sidestepped, circling them, and the rest of the dogs did, too. Brodie spun uneasily, keeping Darkly in front of himself. "You guys, with all your little twinkling lights, you're good dogs, right?"

Brodie and Tuck, still moving to try and keep an eye on the dogs, didn't answer.

"Well," Darkly went on, finally coming to a stop. He lowered his head and looked up at Brodie. "We're the bad dogs."

"What do you want?" Brodie asked, turning quickly to lift his lip at one of the other dogs, who had crept too close to his rear.

"Oh, nothing much," he said, a tease in his voice. "Just a little . . . snack."

One of the other dogs, a little spotted one, darted in suddenly, snapping his quick teeth at Tuck's haunches. Tuck spun, snarling, and backed him up.

"Back off, Thump," the leader growled. "I get first taste. You know that."

"Aw, come on, Darkly, there's plenty! Look at all their—"

"I said back off!" Darkly snarled, and Thump did. Quick.

"Leave us alone," Tuck warned, and his voice was harder than Brodie had ever heard it.

Darkly moved in closer, his head low, his black eyes on Tuck.

"No," he said, and his voice was a hungry growl.

And then he lunged.

All that furry muscle tightened up and then surged forward, right toward Tuck.

Tuck stumbled backward, his teeth flashing, and Brodie leapt forward to help.

It seemed to be exactly what Darkly had been expecting.

In one snakelike motion he swung toward Brodie, catching him off-balance and off guard.

His powerful legs shot his meaty body like a bullet at Brodie, jaws first.

Brodie tried to backpedal, but Darkly was too fast and Brodie's paws slid on the pavement.

Darkly's teeth sank into his shoulder.

No.

His teeth sank into . . . *him.*

It was like nothing he'd ever felt.

His teeth sank deep, and a high, ripping whimper was torn from Brodie's throat. But it didn't feel like pain, this bite. It felt far worse than pain.

It felt like every good thing ever was gone forever. It felt like every last ray of sunlight was lost to shadow. It felt like every laugh from his boy's mouth was turned to sobs. It felt like his tail would never, *could* never, wag again. New words came into his mind like hard slaps: *Despair. Hopelessness. Misery.*

Brodie didn't have a body anymore. He didn't have a body that could hurt.

But he had a spirit. He had a soul. Oh, yes. And that evil dog sank his teeth right into it. And took a piece.

He sank his teeth in even deeper and shook his mighty neck, rattling Brodie's whole body. A miserable howl moaned from his mouth.

Then Darkly let go.

He stepped back, his tail wagging, his black eyes aglow. Around him circled two little golden lights. Lights that hadn't been there a moment before.

Brodie knew without being told that they were his. That dog had taken a bit of his soul.

Darkly licked his lips, and his great body quivered.

"Oh, yeah," he said. "That was *good*. You got so much in you still, freshy. So much good stuff."

Brodie was still panting from the agony of what had been taken from him. He looked for Tuck. He was on the ground, fighting and struggling but being held down by the other three dogs.

"Leave him alone!" Tuck cried, snapping at his attackers but getting only air.

"Is it our turn, Darkly? Huh?" asked one of the dogs holding down Tuck. "Can we take some?" It was a medium-sized dog, black with a brown chest, with a short-docked tail and stiff upright triangle ears.

"Not yet, Smoker," Darkly answered, and his voice was dreamy. "I gotta get mine first." His eyes rolled back and he howled, a triumphant, satisfied howl. "Oh, it feels *so good*."

He lifted his nose toward the sky and closed his eyes. He was savoring the taste of Brodie's soul. He turned a slow circle, licking his lips, his eyes still closed.

At the same time, Brodie saw one of the dogs holding Tuck slip off him, snarling at Thump, who had lowered his bared teeth toward Tuck, hoping to sneak a bite.

"He said to wait!" the dog snapped, and Thump backed off, lips raised in a greedy show of teeth.

Brodie saw their chance.

And he ran.

Not away from the dogs. Toward them.

With the two dogs glaring at each other, only one dog was left on Tuck. Brodie barreled into him with everything he had, lowering his shoulder and ramming him with so much force that he flew through the air and rolled when he hit the ground.

Tuck popped up, teeth ready. But the numbers were not in their favor for a fight.

"Run!" Brodie shouted.

You never had to ask Tuck to run twice.

They ran.

"Get 'em!" Darkly howled.

Brodie started in the lead but Tuck was beside him in no time, and then past him, his legs stretching and feet flying. Man, that dog could *run*.

The houses blurred as they ran; then the houses gave way to vacant lots and dark warehouses and empty parking lots. They were out of the area where people lived. There were shadows here, and broken windows, and piles of snow-draped garbage.

Aiden! Brodie thought frantically. They were getting farther and farther away from him. If they went too far, he might not be able to find him again. A word flashed in his mind: *lost*. It was a bad word. It was something he didn't want to be. His feet slowed, doubt slowing his strides. But then he heard running paws too close behind him, felt a mouth snap at his tail and barely miss. He remembered the feeling of Darkly's teeth tearing into his soul. And then he ran *hard*, harder than he ever had before, hard enough to leave, for a while, his doubt behind.

He looked back. Their pursuers were still there, charging after them, determined. But Tuck and Brodie were faster. Tuck especially. They'd given themselves a big lead, almost half a block. But the dark-eyed dogs weren't giving up.

A brick building flashed beside them, full of boarded-up windows. A corner was just ahead.

“Turn here!” Brodie shouted. “Go around the corner!” He didn’t want to get any farther from Aiden than he had to.

Tuck reached the corner and took it tight, almost slipping but keeping his feet under him and rocketing off like lightning in their new direction. Brodie did his best to follow. He wasn’t as graceful as Tuck, maybe, or as quick, but he made it.

Once he got up to top speed he looked back, checking to see if the dogs had made it around the corner yet.

But he couldn’t see them. Had they stopped chasing?

He *almost* started to slow down.

We just need to lose these dogs, he thought, his legs churning, *and then we can—*

WHAM!

Something slammed into his hind legs from the side, knocking him off his feet. He tumbled and rolled and then skidded to a halt.

It didn’t hurt—not having an actual body can be a good thing, sometimes—but he had to shake his head to clear his thoughts.

Just in time, he saw the dog coming at him. It was Thump, the little spotted one. Somehow he’d caught up to him. He was coming at Brodie again, teeth bared in an ugly snarl.

Just as Brodie jumped to his feet to fight him off, the other three appeared. They came charging right *out of* the wall of the building next to him, their soulless eyes and flashing teeth and running legs flying right through the bricks like they weren't there.

Brodie didn't even have time to process what he'd just seen.

The two smaller ones slowed as they saw him, spreading out to cut off his escape. But Darkly didn't miss a step. He thundered right at Brodie, hungry mouth open wide for a bite. When he was a few paces away he leapt with all four paws, flying like a nightmare at Brodie's throat. There was no time to run. Nowhere to hide. No way to stop him.

Brodie flinched, bracing for the impact.

It never came.

Instead, out of the corner of his eye, he saw a black blur rocket out of nowhere, shooting right past him. The blur collided with Darkly's ribs in midair, deflecting the big dog and sending him rolling into two of his cronies.

The blur, of course, was Tuck. Tuck had come back for him.

Because Tuck? He was exactly the kind of dog who will always come back for his friends, no matter how black-eyed the beast that chases them.

He shot out of the night like a cannonball and saved Brodie from Darkly's soul-snatching teeth. Well, for a second, anyway.

Tuck barely slowed down. He stumbled sideways for a few steps, recovering from his collision with Darkly, but he never stopped moving. He spun around and surged away again in the direction they'd been running.

"Come on, Brodie!" he shouted, looking over his shoulder to make sure Brodie was following. "Get moving!"

Brodie got moving. He heard wild jaws snapping at him as he got up to speed but none got him, and soon he was trailing right behind Tuck's sprinting legs. As he ran he thought desperately about the way they'd caught up to him, how he'd seen them materialize right out of the solid brick wall.

"No more turning!" he called out when he was close enough for Tuck to hear him. "Keep going straight!"

They ran past one corner. Then another. He was losing track of where they were, of which direction Aiden's house was in. Had they gone past it? Were they still running away from it?

They approached another corner, but this one was different. The road they were running on didn't keep going . . . it met another road, but then stopped in a T intersection, giving them only two options: turn left or right. But Brodie knew that turning only gave the dark dogs another chance to catch up to them.

"Which way?" Tuck asked as they got closer.

Brodie ran a few more steps, thinking, then squinted straight ahead.

The street they were on *did* end, the way blocked by large, lightless brick buildings. But looking closer, he saw a passageway between them, a dark little break between the bricks. *Alley*, his mind told him, and he knew it was their best bet.

"Keep going straight!" he answered. "Do you see the little alleyway?"

"Got it!" Tuck replied, and they charged together across the street and into the shadowy alley.

The asphalt in the alley was grease-stained and strewn with litter. The snow along the edges was filthy gray slush. The walls were close, blocking out most of the light from the streetlights behind and the stars above, turning their path into a valley of shadows. Their pursuers were a ways behind but still coming, their lifeless legs just as tireless as Brodie's and Tuck's.

But, running straight, Brodie knew they'd get away eventually.

Until, that is, they hit the dead end.

Without warning the alley widened out into a big square lot. There was a truck parked to one side, and a couple of fragrant dumpsters on the other. But all around the space were walls. Four solid brick walls. They had doors—big, metal doors that rolled up to open, like garage doors—but they were all closed.

Tuck and Brodie ran to the end of the lot, but stopped short. The only way out was back the way they'd come—and that way was blocked by the four running dogs who were getting closer to them with each second.

When Darkly and his thugs saw them there, stopped

and surrounded by walls, they slowed down to a sure, victorious walk.

Darkly licked at his teeth. Brodie's own soul lights still circled around him, reflecting off the shiny all-blackness of his gloating eyes.

Brodie and Tuck were trapped.

CHAPTER SEVEN

"We gotta get outta here," Tuck panted, pacing furiously, looking at the walls all around them. He jumped up against the back wall again and again. That wall was lower, and didn't seem to be a part of a building like the others. But it was still too tall to jump.

"It's no use," Brodie said, turning reluctantly to face the approaching dogs. "We're gonna have to fight our way out."

"Fight our way out? Against all four of them? No chance, buddy."

"Maybe. But no choice, either, Tuck."

Tuck turned a few more anxious circles, nose sniffing and eyes racing. The other dogs were almost with them now in the walled lot.

Then, finally, he stopped pacing. He came to rest standing beside Brodie, so that their shoulders touched. He stretched his jaw, stilled his tail.

"All right," he said, and his voice was tense but no longer panicked. "Here's the plan. We split up. I'll go after the fast one—that spotted mutt. I'll pin him. First chance you get, slip past the other three and scram. You're way faster than them. You'll make it. Once you're out, I'll try to shake 'em, too. We can meet back at that park we started in."

Tuck looked at Brodie, and he said his next words, low and serious, into Brodie's eyes.

"If I'm not at the park, go on without me. Go find your boy. Do what you gotta do."

"No, Tuck, listen, I . . ."

"No time to argue, buddy."

And then Tuck? Tuck squared his shoulders to face the oncoming beasts. He shook the quivers out of his neck.

And Brodie? Brodie thought about arguing for a moment, but then blew out a deep breath and did the same.

Those two bravehearted dogs? They were ready.

Together, they waited to battle for their souls.

But then, a hissed voice: "Good *lord*. Are you two *really* this *stupid*?"

Tuck and Brodie both jumped in surprise.

Their heads snapped back to find the voice that had spoken from somewhere behind them.

A cat sat behind a garbage can against the wall at their backs. She was scrawny and rib-showing thin, her long hair a patchy mix of brown and black and white. She had one furry ear that pivoted around, listening. There was just a scarred, pink little stump where the other ear should have been.

For a second, Brodie couldn't figure out how she could see them, and how they could hear her.

And then he saw the faint glow shimmering around her fur, and the little golden lights circling her. There were only four or five, but they were there.

The cat was dead. Just like them.

She blinked slowly and yawned.

She looked tough. And bored.

"What . . . what . . . do you mean?" Brodie asked.

"Shhh. They don't know *I'm* here, Fido. Be cool. Look at *them*."

Brodie reluctantly turned his eyes back to the four dogs, who had finally strutted into the open space and had spread out, still coming toward them. Their black eyes glittered hungrily as they came, and their dangling tongues licked at their lips.

"Do you mutts *actually* think you're *trapped*?" the cat whispered. "You *gotta* be brand-new or super stupid. Or both. Yeah. Probably both."

Brodie ignored her insults. The bad dogs were only getting closer, and the cat's words had given him some hope.

"We're not trapped?" Brodie asked quietly, his eyes still on the dogs. "I'm seeing a lot of walls, cat."

"Sure. And if you had *bodies*, those walls'd be a problem, wouldn't they?"

And then, in a flash, Brodie got it. He remembered the dogs appearing out of the brick wall to catch up to them, and it clicked in his brain.

"Tuck," he whispered. "These dogs can run through walls. I saw it."

"Great," he answered, his throat growling at the attackers. "That don't help *us* much, buddy."

"If they can," Brodie replied, "then *we* can."

Tuck looked at him. His tail got right to wagging.

"How do we do it?" Brodie asked the cat, backing up toward the wall.

"What do you mean, *how*? These walls couldn't stop you if they tried." From the corner of his eye he saw the cat stand up and stretch, her eyes closed in pleasure. "I mean, you *do* know you're dead, right?"

"Well, yeah, but . . ."

"Hold on a sec," the cat interrupted, and then disappeared backward through the wall. Brodie's mouth dropped open. The cat had just sauntered right back through the bricks and out of sight. Brodie blinked sideways at the wall, then turned back to face the dogs.

"Where'd she go?" Tuck asked, but before Brodie could answer, Darkly cut in.

"Nowhere to go, fellas," he said, his voice smug with satisfaction. They were only a few feet away now, moving slow to block their escape, their eyes hungrily following the little lights swirling around Brodie and Tuck.

One of the others spoke up, talking under his breath to Darkly but loud enough for Brodie to hear.

"Hey, boss, why don't they just . . ."

"Zip it, Skully," Darkly warned. "They're *fresh*, remember? And we're gonna teach 'em a bit about how this world works, ain't we?" They all closed in a few steps more. "Mmmm. I think I'm gonna start with the ugly black one this time. See how *his* soul tastes."

"Aw, save some for the rest of us, boss!" Thump protested.

"Don't worry," Darkly reassured him. "These two is so fresh, there's plenty for everybody. I just get mine first, got it?"

"Well, then, who's second?" Skully asked. "Me, right?"

"No way, Skully! I been here longer! Right, Darkly? I'm next, right?"

"You think I care, Smoker?" Darkly snapped.

"Well, *I* care," Smoker whined. "I don't wanna get cut out like last time!"

Tuck and Brodie stood there, listening to them argue over who got second shot at their eternal souls.

From behind them, Brodie saw a faint glow behind the garbage can. He snuck a look and saw that the cat had stuck her scarred head back through the wall.

"You guys had enough fun?" she whispered. "Or you wanna get out of here? Follow me. I think I got this figured." Her head disappeared, then reappeared a moment later. "Oh. First time can be tricky, I guess, especially for idiots. Just remember: The wall is there, but *you* ain't. You'll only hit the wall if you *expect* to hit it. Don't think about it. Just walk through it. Like it's one of them doggy doors, or whatever. You'll pop right through." With these words, the cat disappeared again.

Brodie and Tuck looked at each other.

"What do you think?" Tuck asked.

"I think we've got no other options."

Tuck wagged his tail.

"Let's give it a shot, buddy."

Brodie turned back to Darkly and his gang. They were a little too close for comfort.

“I’d worry less about taking turns on our souls,” he said, cutting into their argument. “And worry more about that angel behind you.”

All four heads snapped quickly around.

Because those dogs? They were bad, but they weren’t the smartest pups in obedience school.

Brodie and Tuck spun around. And without time to think about it, they jumped at the wall.

To Brodie, it felt crazy. Jumping straight into a wall? But he’d seen the other dogs do it. And he’d just watched the cat do it. So he followed the cat’s advice: He didn’t think about it. He just jumped.

Right at the wall.

When his paws hit pavement again, he was on the other side of the wall, on a sidewalk, with a road in front of him and a supposedly solid brick wall at his back. Tuck was beside him, and his whole *body* was wagging.

“That was *awesome*,” Tuck crowed. Then he looked back at the wall. “But we better run.”

“This way!” the cat called from up the street. She was running flat out, her one ear back and her tail down. There wasn’t time to think about it. They bounded after her.

The street was busier than the ones they’d been on so far. A car passed them going the other way, and up ahead, there was a line of vehicles stopped at a red traffic light.

They gained on the cat quick. She was fast, but she was still a cat.

Behind them they could hear the snarling and growling of four very hungry, very angry, very dead dogs.

"What's the plan?" Brodie asked the cat, pulling up beside her.

"That truck," she answered, her eyes still straight ahead.

Brodie looked. One of the vehicles stopped at the light was a truck . . . one of those big ones that people use to haul stuff around. The back of it, though, wasn't a big metal box like most of them were. It was just a big, flat wooden platform, empty and waiting. It was perfect. But it was also pretty high up. Higher than Brodie could jump, for sure.

"How we gonna get up there?"

"Just follow me, pooch."

Brodie looked back.

Running at the cat's speed, the trio was losing ground to the dogs at their heels. They were gonna get caught before they even got to the truck.

"We're not gonna make it!" Brodie warned.

The cat lowered her head and pumped her legs harder, trying to squeeze more speed out of them.

It didn't work.

Tuck looked back over his shoulder, sizing up their pursuers. Then he looked back to the cat.

"C'mon," he said. "Let's speed this up a bit." He drifted toward the cat, his mouth open. The cat saw him coming.

"Don't you da—" But the cat didn't have a chance to finish her threat. Tuck grabbed the back of her neck in his teeth and scooped her right up in mid-stride, holding her dangling from his jaws as he ran. He never missed a step. The cat howled and hissed and thrashed, but Tuck just shook her a bit and ran harder.

Up ahead, the stoplight turned green. The line of cars started crawling into motion, their red taillights blinking off car by car as they began to move forward: the first car . . . the second car . . . the third . . . and then the flatbed truck.

"How are we getting up there?" Brodie asked again.

The cat growled stubbornly in Tuck's jaws and swiped at him fruitlessly with her claws. The truck rumbled as it began to move forward.

"Come on!" Brodie shouted. "Do you have a plan or not?"

"The parked car!" the cat finally spat out. "Use the car!"

Brodie saw it. Parked on the side of the road, right next to the flatbed truck. Well, right next to it right then . . . but the truck was pulling a little farther away from it with every step.

"Got it, Tuck?" Brodie asked.

"Yep, buddy. We got this." He surged ahead, the cat still bouncing around in his clenched teeth.

The truck was picking up speed. It was halfway past the car now.

They buckled down, sprinting hard to make it before it was too late.

Tuck got there first. He sprang from the street to the car's trunk, then up to its roof, barely slowing at all. A couple of steps along the roof of the car and then he leapt, his body stretching and soaring through the streetlight glow.

Tuck? He was quite a sight, flying sleek and silky through the night, his soul glittering all around him, his mouth full of furious cat. Quite a sight. Quite a dog.

He landed gracefully atop the truck's flatbed and skidded to a halt.

Brodie was right behind him. A determined jump up to the trunk, not as effortless as Tuck's, but he made it. Then to the roof, losing speed but not taking his eyes off the truck. It was almost past him now and still picking up speed.

"Jump, Brodie!" Tuck called. Brodie jumped with everything he had, stretching his front paws toward the accelerating truck.

He hung in the air. For a moment, the world was soundless.

It was close. Man, it was close.

It would have been tempting for a watching angel to help him. But none did.

His front paws touched down on the stained wood of the truck's bed. His back paws fell just short but his momentum carried him forward, sending him tumbling across the flatbed. He came to an awkward stop a paw's length away from rolling right off the other side.

He looked up at Tuck, who was standing over him with his tail wagging fierce, and sound came back to Brodie's ears: the roar of the truck's engine, a distant honking of some car's horn, the furious barking of four demonic dogs running hopelessly after the truck he was now riding.

"Nice jump, buddy."

"Thanks," Brodie said, standing up and shaking his head.

The cat still dangled from Tuck's mouth. She wasn't squirming anymore. She was just hanging there, her few little soul lights circling her sulking head. Her good ear was pointed straight back. The fur all over her skinny body was puffed out in fury. Her eyes smoldered with anger so clear Brodie could almost *smell* it.

He didn't remember much about his life yet. But he was pretty sure he'd never seen an animal madder than that cat looked, hanging out of Tuck's slobbery mouth.

"Put. Me. Down."

"Uh, yeah, I'd put her down, Tuck."

Tuck opened his mouth and the cat fell to the truck bed with a thump. Tuck stood there, wagging his tail and grinning, like he was expecting a "Thank you."

The cat rose up on her paws, arched her back, and turned to face him.

"If you weren't already dead," she snarled, low and growly, "I'd kill you."

Tuck's wagging slowed.

"What? Why?"

Brodie stepped between them, toward the end of the truck bed. The truck was moving along pretty fast now, and he walked slowly to keep his balance.

The dogs were close—only a few running strides behind the truck, really—but the truck was picking up speed and starting to leave them behind. And they had no way to get up to where Brodie stood watching them.

They'd made it.

The dogs weren't giving up, though. They ran on, their teeth bared and their eyes flashing angrily. Darkly still had Brodie's soul lights glowing around him.

"We'll get you!" he roared. "We'll find you and we'll rip all that shine right off you!"

Tuck joined Brodie at the back of the truck, his tail beating happily. They watched as the dogs fell farther and farther behind the truck, slowing from a snarling sprint to a stubborn jog.

"He seems upset," Tuck said.

"Yeah," Brodie agreed. The big yellow dog with the devilish black eyes was falling more behind by the second. But his eyes never left them where they stood on the back of the truck.

"Golden retrievers are known for their friendliness, relaxed demeanor, and generous good nature," Tuck said. He cocked his head at Brodie. "But maybe that's just the ones that are alive."

Brodie didn't answer.

He was remembering the pain, that unbearable agony, of having a piece of his soul torn away.

And he was looking at that demon dog's unblinking eyes and his determined, tireless run. He wasn't gonna stop, Brodie knew.

That dog—that soulless, snarling hellhound—was a predator.

And Brodie's soul was the prey.

CHAPTER EIGHT

The cat sat in the middle of the truck bed, her body a tight ball of anger. She strained to lick clean the spot on her back where Tuck had held her in his teeth.

"Great thinking on the truck," Tuck said to her. "And you're welcome for the ride, by the way."

The cat pulled back her lips, showing her sharp white teeth.

"If you ever do that again, dog breath, I'll scratch your eyes out."

"You can't scratch a ghost's eyes out." Tuck grinned, all smile and wag.

The cat narrowed her eyes. Her tail whipped furiously.

"You sure about that?"

Tuck looked nervously sideways at Brodie.

"She can't, can she?"

"How long do we have to stay up here?" Brodie asked, changing the subject. He looked back at the dogs, still visible in the distance, running after them.

"Until they stop chasing us, smart stuff," the cat answered. "Or until we hit another red light. Better start praying *that* doesn't happen too soon." She looked past Brodie to glare at their pursuers. "They ain't gonna get tired, you know. So you may as well settle in. We could be on this dump till morning."

Brodie shifted uneasily. He could feel the truck pulling him farther and farther away from his boy. He turned a nervous circle and eyed the dogs chasing them, waiting for them to disappear so he could hop off and find Aiden.

Because Brodie? His heart had a compass needle that never lost its way.

"No," he said. "I can't wait that long."

"What's the rush, dog?" the cat asked, stretching and lying down. "This truck is taking us away from those mutts that were just *dyin'* to tear your soul to pieces. Relax and enjoy the ride."

"I can't."

The cat's eyes narrowed.

"Why not?"

Brodie hesitated. The cat had saved their skins, there was no doubt about that. But he wasn't sure how much he really wanted to trust her.

"We just got here," he began. "Well, we just got *back* here. From . . . that other place, ya know? And I've . . . got something I need to do."

The cat blinked.

"Something you need to *do*?" she asked. Her voice had lost some of its angry edge. "There's nothing you can *do* here, dog. You can *watch*. You can *want*. You can *lose*. But you can't *do* nothing."

Brodie swallowed. He listened to the rumble of the truck that was pulling them through the night. He was looking for words, and trying to calm the tremble that the cat's words had sent into his heart.

"I have to," he said at last.

The cat gave him a slow, bored blink.

"Huh. Well, what is it, then? What hopeless thing do you gotta *not* do down here?"

Brodie looked up at the stars for just a second, closing his eyes to bring back the memory of Aiden's face, of his arms tight around him.

"I have to find my boy. I have to make sure he's okay."

"Your boy?" the cat sneered. "And what are you gonna do if he's not okay?"

Brodie looked her right in her cold, feline eyes.

"Then I'll save him."

The cat looked at Brodie for a long moment. Then she blinked and looked out at the night.

"You're such an idiot," she said. "I should've let 'em have you. It would have been quicker that way, at least."

Brodie's ears drooped.

"Hey, knock it off," Tuck cut in. "Don't listen to her, buddy. She don't know what she's talking about."

"Really?" the cat shot back. "And you do, brainless?" Her fur bristled. "You can't help the living. And they can't help you. Trust me on that, pooch."

Brodie stepped anxiously from foot to foot, licking his lips. He looked at Tuck, then back at the dogs that were just distant dots by then, then to the parked cars they were passing.

Because that cat's words? They shook him up something awful. They did. They shook him up in a way that, just for a moment, made him doubt everything. Even himself.

But then . . . then, they just *didn't*. That's the only way to describe it. It all came back to that compass needle in Brodie's heart, you see. You could shake it up all you wanted. But Brodie's heart was the kind that never gets lost. Even when it didn't know where it was. His needle spun; then it came back to his true north. Aiden.

He stopped his pacing. He clenched his teeth tight.

"I'm gonna try," Brodie said. "That's all I know. I'm gonna try. I've *gotta* try."

That cat gave him a long look that Brodie couldn't quite read.

"Fine. Go ahead and try. But you're gonna have to ride up here for a while, anyway. You know, unless you want your soul to be Darkly's next chew toy."

Brodie knew she was right. He knew that getting into it with those dogs would only slow him down and make it even harder to get back to Aiden. He tried to remember what the angel had said, tried to remember the bigger truth. If he just waited until they were out of sight of those dogs—even if the truck just went around a corner, maybe—he could jump off and cut back to Aiden. That's all he had to do. Take a breath. See the big picture. Wait.

He turned his head to look back at the cat.

"My name's Brodie," he said. "And his name is Tuck."

The cat blinked at him and yawned, her tongue curling dramatically.

"Fascinating," she replied.

"What's yours?"

"What's my what?"

"Your, uh, name."

The cat licked her paw and scrubbed behind her ear. Brodie thought she wasn't going to answer, but between licks she muttered, "Patsy."

"Patsy?" Tuck exclaimed. "Your name's *Patsy*?"

Patsy stopped her bathing and fixed Tuck with a seething glare.

"Yeah. Something wrong with that?"

"Nah," Tuck said. "It's just such a . . . *cute* name, is all."

"Well, *I* didn't pick it." She gave her chest a last couple licks, then straightened up and looked back and forth between Tuck and Brodie. Her eyes followed the glowing paths of their circling soul lights.

"Man," she said quietly, her eyes sharp and her voice far away. "You mutts got *so much* shine. It's been a long time since I seen that much soul in one place." Her tongue slid along her lips, then she shook her head and looked away.

Brodie looked back behind them. His tail leapt into a high wag, and he jumped to his feet. The truck had picked up speed while they'd been talking. The dark dogs were nearly gone, nearly out of sight in the darkness.

"We lost 'em," he said. "Time to hop off."

The cat craned her neck, looking back down the road.

"I wouldn't jump yet. They're still back there. Best to wait until sunrise. It ain't too long."

"Why sunrise?"

"Those hellhounds chasing us. Their kind don't move around much when the sun's up. Once your soul's gone, you just feel more like sticking to the shadows. Sunlight, daytime, people and animals moving around . . . it all just feels too *alive*, you know? The soulless just don't *fit*."

Behind Patsy, Tuck was stomping his paws on the truck bed. He scratched at it with his claws. He raised up on his hind legs, then brought both front paws down on the truck bed with all the weight of his body. Brodie had been ignoring it for as long as he could.

"Tuck!" he snapped. "What are you doing?"

"I don't get it," he said. "So we jumped right through that wall. But here we are on this truck."

"Careful," the cat said, her voice bored.

"See what I'm saying?" Tuck went on. "Why can we touch this truck?" He pawed stubbornly at the truck bed beneath them.

"Careful," the cat said again, yawning.

"It doesn't make sense, though! If we can go straight through a wall, we should go straight through . . ."

Tuck didn't get a chance to finish his thought. In mid-sentence, he disappeared. He dropped right down through the truck bed. The last Brodie saw of him was a pair of wide eyes and a couple of flapping ears.

Patsy rolled her eyes.

"I warned him."

"Where'd he go?"

The cat pointed with her chin toward the road behind them. Brodie turned and saw Tuck, sitting in the road, shaking his head and looking around.

He spied them driving away and hopped up to chase them.

"Hey!" he hollered. "Wait up!"

"He's not, like, super smart, is he?" Patsy asked. "I mean, even for a dog."

"Tuck!" Brodie shouted, stepping to the very back of the truck.

Tuck was running full out but the truck was really moving now, and he was falling behind by the second.

"He's not gonna catch us!" Brodie said.

"Nah. Probably not." Patsy yawned behind him.

"What can we do?"

"I dunno. Shout good-bye and count our blessings?"

"Seriously, Patsy!"

Tuck's legs were pumping, his tongue flapping, but he was getting smaller and smaller and farther and farther away.

"Geez, if you *have* to stay with that half-wit, just jump off and join him."

"Jump off? A moving truck?"

Brodie looked down at the asphalt whizzing by beneath them. He hopped from foot to foot. He brought his claws right up to the edge.

"Brodie!" Tuck called.

Brodie wiggled his rear, getting ready to jump.

"You really gonna jump?" Patsy asked.

"Yeah."

"Here, then. Give me a ride."

"Huh? What do you m—"

Without warning, Patsy's weight landed with a thump on his shoulders. Her claws dug into his back, but just enough to hold on. The force of her hitting him threw him off-balance and he lurched forward. He tried to pull back but it was no use. He tumbled off the back of the truck and plummeted toward the street.

CHAPTER NINE

Brodie landed with a skidding thump, his paws scrambling frantically to keep up with his body. Patsy leapt off his back while he fought to keep his balance. His paws lost the race and he rolled across the asphalt and came to rest in the middle of the road. The truck was rumbling away from them, its taillights glowing red.

Patsy stood calmly beside him, lazily licking at her shoulder. Tuck came running up.

"Epic wipeout!"

"Thanks," Brodie said, standing up and flexing all his muscles. Despite the high-speed crash onto cold winter asphalt, he felt totally fine.

Being a dead, bodiless spirit dog? It's not *all* bad.

"So, uh, what now?" Tuck asked, looking around. There was more traffic on the street now, more cars passing them without seeing them. The horizon was starting to glow a pale yellow.

"Well, we don't hang around here," Patsy answered. "Those hellhounds could be right behind us."

"No," Brodie said. "They're pretty far back. They're heading our way, but just walking."

Tuck cocked his head.

"How do you know that?"

Brodie blinked. He looked at Tuck, then away down the

road toward where he knew, just somehow *knew*, that Darkly and his gang were moving steadily toward them.

"I don't know," he said.

Patsy was looking closely at him, her eyes narrowed.

"Wait a minute. Darkly had a bit of glow on him, didn't he? Where'd he get it?"

"Well . . . from *me*. He . . . ripped it off me, or something." He paused, remembering the horrible, heart-shaking agony of his soul being torn. "It was *terrible*."

"Well, great," Patsy spat. Her hair rose and she stared intensely back toward wherever the hellhounds were, coming toward them. "He's got some of your soul, you idiot. You're connected now. You can feel him. And he can feel you."

"So?"

"So? So he can follow you." The cat paced, her body tight and her hair still raised. "Quick. Feel him out. How far are we talking here? How much time do we have?"

Brodie closed his eyes. And, yeah, there it was. He could *feel* Darkly. Feel the thin, ghostly connection between them. He could feel his hungry presence in the distance. He felt it in his head, felt it with his thoughts the way you sniff at a faint smell to figure out what it is and where it's coming from.

"He's . . . he's . . . I don't know, kind of a long way off. Nowhere close."

"Okay. But not running?"

Brodie felt again, concentrating.

"No, he's just walking, I think. Even slower now. He feels . . . um . . . he's feeling . . ." He squeezed his eyes tight, focusing on the feeling and finding new words to describe it. "He feels restless, and . . . uneasy? He's looking for . . . someplace dark? Yeah. That's it. They stopped walking."

He opened his eyes, wagging his tail at his success.

"Right," Patsy said thoughtfully. "It's almost sunrise. They'll want to hole up until dark. But then they'll be right on us. No way they're letting shine like yours get away."

"Okay," Brodie said. "We'll just get to my boy before nighttime, then. No problem."

Patsy gave him a look scornful enough to have dried up Brodie's spit, if he'd had any.

"Yeah," she said. "No problem. We better move."

Tuck looked at her.

"You're coming with us?"

Patsy yawned.

"Yeah. I guess."

Tuck's mouth popped open into a grin and his tail beat a steady wag.

"Really? Why?"

"Well, let's see. I'm small, and you're big. I'm down to about zero soul, and you're filthy with it. I'm bored, and you're . . . amusing. Besides, I'm dead. What else am I gonna do?"

Tuck's tail wagged harder. He gave Patsy a happy lick.

"Cool! This'll be fun! Welcome to our—" His words were cut short by a hiss and a batting paw.

"Easy, dogface. Don't talk me out of it. You two morons need me a heckuva lot more than I need you."

Tuck retreated, his tail between his legs but his eyes still cheerful.

Patsy looked to Brodie, her tail swishing irritably. "Which way, smart stuff? The clock's ticking."

Luckily, Brodie didn't think they had to head back toward the waiting hellhounds. He figured that the chase of the night before—first on foot, then on the truck—had been kind of two sides of a triangle, and by where the sun rose and from some faint stirrings of memory, he was able to figure out what he thought was the right general direction for them to head in to get back to where they'd started. They didn't waste any time.

The world woke up around them as they walked. People walked out of houses and got into cars. Birds sang and flew from tree to tree. Cats and dogs and squirrels went about their business of chasing, slinking, eating, barking. All those silly, pointless, wonderful things that living animals do. The three dead animals walked through it all, surrounded by it, but hopelessly separate. None of the barks were for them, none of the people stooped to pet them, squirrels didn't even bother running away when Tuck bounded up to them, barking. They were worse than invisible.

And being invisible and ignored in a bright world full of life? It's not a great feeling. Brodie couldn't help but remember the angel's words: *You're done with that world now. And it's done with you.*

To fill the silence between them—and the loneliness within himself—Brodie peppered Patsy with questions while they walked.

"So . . . how does this all work? Like, why did Tuck fall through the truck like that?"

"It ain't that complicated," Patsy said. "We ain't actually here, right? I mean, not our *bodies*. Those are rotting away somewhere, feeding the worms. So we can go through walls, fences, trucks, you name it. But our souls have enough to them, enough memory of being around, that we can kinda make ourselves real enough for us to move around. Like . . . we don't just fall right through the ground, right? And since you *thought* you could jump up on the truck, you *could*. But once you thought about *not* standing on the truck, you couldn't. Get it?"

"Nope," Tuck said cheerfully, snapping pointlessly at a butterfly that fluttered past.

"I'm shocked."

"So, we kinda choose what's real?" Brodie asked. "We can choose what to touch?"

"More or less. But it costs you. Every time you really *touch* the world, every time you make yourself real enough to *do* something—like jump on a truck—it costs you a little bit of your soul. Even walking down this sidewalk right now, all this touching of the world . . . it's taking a little of our souls, just a drop at a time."

"But I could, like, bite something, if I really wanted to?" Brodie asked.

"I guess. If you try, you could make yourself a little *more* real, real enough to touch stuff and bite stuff and move stuff. But that costs you even more, right? And once you get down to nothing, *you're* nothing. You're stuck."

Brodie walked on a bit, thinking.

"But those dogs. They didn't have any shine. How can they still move around? How come they can touch the sidewalk and run, if they don't have any soul left to spend?"

"The hellhounds? I dunno. No one does, maybe. Maybe it's *because* they're stuck, like they're part of this world again. In a way, they're kinda *real* again. But it ain't no way to be. Trust me."

"Why are they called hellhounds?" Tuck cut in.

"Who knows? They're evil. They're nasty. They're dead and they ain't never getting to heaven. The name kinda works, I guess."

"Is it just dogs? I mean, are there such things as hell*cats*?"

"Sure, there's hellcats. I even ran into a hell*bird* once. Now *that* was a creature I'd rather not meet again, I tell ya. Nasty little thing. No sense of respect."

They came up to a busy intersection. There was a gas station and a stoplight and a couple of the restaurants where Brodie remembered people could drive through in their cars and get food. He sniffed at the air, savoring the greasy, familiar smell of hot food.

"That costs ya, too, ya know," Patsy said.

"What?"

"Smelling like that. You ain't *thinking*, pooch. You just made your nose real enough to pick up smells in the air. Keep doing that, and your soul will be gone before you know it."

Brodie's heart sank.

"Seriously? But . . . how do I stop it?"

"Same way smart stuff over there fell through the truck. Just stop expecting to smell—which is the same as *trying* to smell, really—and then you won't anymore. You can only touch stuff—with your paws, your teeth, your nose—that you *try* to touch."

"Wait a sec," Tuck interrupted. "You're saying that if I want to, I can bite stuff? Does this mean I could . . . eat?"

Patsy stared at him.

"Why would you want to eat? You're dead."

Tuck's eyes danced.

"Why would I want to eat? Are you kidding? Eating is my second favorite thing in the world!"

"Let me guess. Your first favorite is being an idiot."

"Nope. It's running. Shows how much *you* know."

"Yeah. I was totally wrong on that one."

But Tuck was already drifting away, over toward a couple of plastic tables outside one of the restaurants. Brodie shot Patsy an impatient look and then followed.

"What are you doing, Tuck? We need to . . ."

"Look," Tuck said, cutting Brodie off. His voice was intense, breathless. "It's *beautiful*."

"What is? We don't have time for this, Tuck."

But Brodie trotted up beside him. And then he saw it. Sitting in the sunshine on one of the table benches, next to a crumpled-up paper bag.

"A french fry," Tuck whispered. His eyes were locked on it, sharp and shiny. "Hey, cat! How do I do this?" he breathed.

Patsy hopped up on the bench beside the french fry. She gave it half a look. She didn't seem nearly as impressed as Tuck.

"You understand that it will literally cost you your soul to eat that, right?" she asked.

"Yeah. Sure. Whatever. Just tell me."

"Can we just keep moving, Tuck?" Brodie cut in. "We're kind of in a hurry, remember?"

Tuck tore his eyes from the french fry long enough to shoot him a desperate look.

"Come on, buddy! We got time for one french fry, right? Just one little fry?"

Brodie looked impatiently up the road, then back to Tuck.

"Fine. Eat the fry. But hurry up."

"Great! Thanks!" He looked back to Patsy, his whole body wagging. "So what do I do?"

"Just concentrate. Look at the fry. Focus on making your teeth, like, *real.* Then bite it. If you want it enough, it'll work. That's it."

Brodie didn't think that wanting it enough was going to be a problem for Tuck. The black dog stepped up to the fry.

His tail stopped wagging. His whole body was tense with concentration. He leaned forward. His mouth opened.

He snapped at the french fry.

It disappeared into his mouth. He jumped, like he was surprised it had worked. He chewed once, twice. His tail started to wag again.

Then the fry dropped right out of his throat. It landed, half-chewed, on the ground. Tuck's tail drooped.

"What happened? I couldn't taste it! And when I swallowed, it just . . . fell through me!"

"You only made your teeth real, meatbrains. If you wanna taste it, you gotta make your tongue real, too. And your throat, if you wanna swallow it. But . . . you're talking major shine loss then, man."

Tuck ignored the warning.

He dropped his head to the fry. He paused, concentrating on the fry. Then, with a slurping gulp, he wolfed it up.

Tuck raised his head, chewing. His tail wagged and his eyes rolled back in his head. He swallowed and grinned.

A few seconds later a chewed-up wad of french fry dropped from his stomach to the ground.

Looking close, Brodie saw one or two of Tuck's little soul lights flicker out and disappear.

But his tail was still wagging.

"You just sold your soul for a french fry," Brodie said.

"Oh, man," Tuck said, his tail wagging so hard that his rump swung from side to side. He licked his lips. "Totally worth it."

Patsy fixed Brodie with a pointed look.

"If you're sticking with this clown, you better find your boy quick. His soul's gonna be gone the first time you walk past a hot dog stand."

"Yeah. Let's get moving," Brodie said, starting off again down the sidewalk. "I'm pretty sure we're heading in the right direction."

"'*Pretty* sure,' mutt? I'm *pretty sure* those hellhounds are gonna chew your soul to shreds once the sun sets. You ain't got a ton of time to just be wandering, you know."

"Thanks for the reminder," Brodie answered over his shoulder. Patsy trotted to catch up. Tuck gave the chewed-up fry one last sniff and joined them. "I think if we keep heading . . ."

His voice cut off when he saw it. It was right in front of them, stopped at a traffic light.

It was big and yellow and it growled as it sat there, waiting for a green light.

A rush of memories washed through his mind.

His tail went to full wag.

"I got it," he said, quickening his step. "I know exactly where we can find Aiden."

CHAPTER TEN

"Really?" Tuck said. "Great! Uh . . . how?"

The light turned green and the monstrous yellow rumbler started to move.

The word had popped into Brodie's head the moment he'd seen it: *bus*. And then: *school.*

And then a stream of memories that started as a trickle and became a flood.

Aiden, leaving in the mornings with a backpack thrown over his shoulder, kissing the top of Brodie's head and saying, "Be good, Brodie." He had hundreds of that memory, almost all the same.

He remembered taking the good-bye and then rushing out the doggy door to the backyard and then squeezing through the hole in the fence and running to catch up to Aiden, barking up into his smiling face. Aiden saying, "No, go home, *Brodie," but not really meaning it. Walking together on the sidewalk, turning a corner or two until the school was there in front of them. Then: Aiden stopping, always under the same shady big-leafed tree, and kneeling down to say good-bye again, but this time adding an extra whisper into Brodie's ear: "Don't wake him up, okay?" Or: "Try to stay out of his way until I get back." Or: "Can't wait till I see you again." They had just been sounds at the time, just noises the boy's mouth made under his pinched, worried eyes, but now he knew what they meant. He had lots of that memory, too. Too many.*

Then: watching him cross the street and join the crowd of kids going into the big building with the bright windows and the fluttering flag. Away.

And then: waiting for him under that tree at the end of the day, waiting to see his pale face and tight-shouldered body come out through the door. And Back.

"School," he answered Tuck. Because in all those memories of the school, in all the ones where he'd watched Aiden walk into the school or waited for him to come out of it, those big yellow buses had always been parked out front, hissing and rumbling and either swallowing kids or spitting them out. "That's where he is. I know it. And we can follow that bus straight there."

"That bus?" Patsy asked. "The one driving away?"

"Yep. Come on!"

Brodie took off running. He heard Tuck's fast footsteps following him, and hoped that Patsy was right behind. He wasn't stopping, though, even if she wasn't. The words from that memory still hummed in his heart: *Can't wait till I see you again.*

I can't wait to see you again, either, Brodie's heart called to his boy, wherever he was. Then, just like Aiden used to say to him, *Try to stay out of his way until I get back.*

They ran.

At first, it was easy. The bus rumbled ahead, got slowed by traffic or a stoplight, and they gained ground. Then it pulled ahead again.

But, after a while, the bus started to pull farther away.

The traffic got lighter, the red lights rarer. There was a long stretch where they almost lost sight of the bus completely.

"We're gonna lose it!" Tuck warned.

"Don't stop!" Brodie answered, his eyes never leaving the grimy yellow of the school bus.

"We're not gonna keep up with it running!" Patsy called out from somewhere behind them.

"You know a better way for us to chase it?" Brodie demanded angrily.

"Actually, yes, dog breath. I do."

Brodie didn't slow down, but he looked back over his shoulder.

"Seriously?"

Ahead, the bus stopped in a long line of cars at a light.

"Perfect!" Patsy exclaimed. "It's time for me to teach you two bozos about car-hopping."

"Car-hopping?"

"Yeah. Invented it myself. You'll love it."

The light turned green, and the traffic jerked car by car back into motion.

"Well, now would be a great time to fill us in."

"All right. Well, you know how we can touch things when we need to—like french fries, if you're an idiot?"

"Yeah, yeah," Brodie said impatiently as the bus rattled into motion in front of them.

"But you know how we can also go right through stuff, like walls? And trucks, if you're an idiot?"

"Yes, Patsy, we know! Get to the point!"

"I'm getting there, pooch. With car-hopping you gotta kinda do both at the same time. You pick a car. Easiest if it's standing still, but it don't gotta be if you're good. You jump through the door, right, but then, while you're *in* the car, you make yourself real, see? Well, real enough to land in the car. Then there you are, riding along in the car. Get it?"

"Got it! Tuck, you get it?"

"I think so, buddy."

"Okay. Let's pick a car, then." Brodie looked at the line of cars. There was a big blue van idling, still waiting for the cars ahead to start moving. "There! That blue one!"

Tuck got there first. He danced his feet nervously, eyeing the blue metal of the van door.

"Go for it!" Brodie said, running up next to him.

"I don't know . . ."

"Come on, brainless," Patsy said. "Just jump through the door like you did the brick wall, then land inside like it's the back of that truck we escaped on. You just gotta switch while you jump is all."

Tuck still hesitated, an anxious whine in his throat.

Then he gathered his legs under him. He shot one unsure look at Brodie. And then he leapt.

Tuck's first shot at car-hopping? It didn't go so great.

His ghostly skull hit that van door and stopped like . . . well, like a skull hitting a van door. There was a faint *dong* and then Tuck fell in a heap into the slushy snow in the gutter.

If Brodie hadn't been so desperate to catch the bus and find his boy, he would have thought it was funny.

Tuck shook his head and looked up at Brodie and Patsy.

"I don't think it works," he said.

"Oh, for God's sake, why am I not surprised?" Patsy growled. In one jump she glided over Tuck's crumpled body and disappeared through the van door. A moment later her face appeared in the window, looking out at them.

"It works, meathead. *You* don't."

The motorcycle that was two cars ahead of the van started moving.

"We gotta get in, Tuck! Come on!"

There was no time to waste. Brodie jumped.

He remembered the brick wall, focused his mind, and flew through the van door.

He saw Patsy's eyes follow him as he flew past her. His brain registered the dirty inside of the van, the gray fabric of the seats, and he concentrated on making himself real. He willed himself to land in the van, just like he'd landed on the back of the flatbed truck.

His paws touched down on the van floor. He blinked. Twisted his head to look at Patsy.

"I did it!"

"Uh-huh. If I had hands I'd clap," she drawled.

Brodie jumped up onto the seat and looked out the window. Tuck was standing on the sidewalk, looking up at them desperately.

"Come on! You can do it, Tuck!"

Tuck jumped.

There was another dull thud. Brodie saw the driver of the van—a woman with big bushy hair and dark sunglasses—furrow her eyebrows and check her rearview mirrors, then shrug and look back to the front.

Tuck was pulling himself out of the gutter again.

"I can't do it!"

"Yes you can! It's just like jumping through the wall, Tuck! You're trying too hard! Just relax and jump in!"

The car in front of the van started forward.

Tuck sprang at them.

Another thud.

"What in the *world*?" the driver muttered, looking in her mirrors again.

"I can't believe this," Patsy muttered.

The van lurched and began moving.

Tuck jumped up out of the slush for the third time and started trotting along beside the van. Brodie knew, though, that he wouldn't be able to keep up forever.

"Listen, Tuck!" Brodie called. "Take a deep breath. Remember the wall. And then just jump, man! You got this!"

Tuck locked eyes with him through the van window.

"Okay," he said. "Okay."

The van was moving faster now.

Tuck jogged a few more steps. His mouth closed in determination. He dug in a bit and picked up speed. Then Tuck jumped.

His black, muscly body glided through the van door.

And then kept going.

He dropped down through the floor of the van. His paws, his legs, his body. Then he stopped.

His feet had hit the icy street beneath the van.

For a moment, Tuck's head was in the van with them, down on the floor. Then it disappeared into the back as the van surged forward.

"Tuck!"

Brodie jumped back to the window, looking for his friend outside. Then he heard his voice. And a bark.

"Hey! Where are you guys?"

The bark came from inside the van.

Brodie put his paws on the back of the seat and looked over it, into the third row behind him.

Tuck's head was in the van between the rows of seats, his neck disappearing down through the floor.

His head was bouncing. And looking up at him.

"Help!"

"What's happening?" Brodie asked.

"He's an idiot. That's what's happening."

"That doesn't help, Patsy!"

"Well, obviously he got the first part right. He went through the van. But he didn't make himself real and land on the floor. He's actually running in the street now, I think. But his head is in here with us. Aren't we lucky."

The van was moving pretty fast by then. Brodie could tell Tuck was straining to keep up.

"I can't keep up much longer! Don't leave me, Brodie! Jump out, guys!"

"No! We have to catch the bus!" Brodie paced back and forth on the seat. He felt the van picking up speed beneath him. "You need to jump up, Tuck."

"What do you mean?"

"This is your last chance. Jump as high as you can. Once the rest of you is all the way up in the van, you gotta make yourself real and land inside. You're gonna have one shot."

"I don't know if I . . ."

"Now, Tuck! Go!"

Tuck's eyes got white and wild. He bared his teeth and growled, a gritty growl of determination that roared up into a bark as he jumped with everything he had.

His body popped up through the floor. It hung for a breath of a moment, then came down, landing in a clumsy pile on the van's backseat.

Tuck grinned up at Brodie, still watching over the backseat.

"I made it, buddy!"

Brodie grinned back.

"Of course, you did. I knew you would," Brodie lied.

Tuck tumbled over the seat and joined Patsy and Brodie. "What now?" he asked.

Brodie craned to look out through the van's windshield. The bus was there, nine or ten cars in front of them.

"We keep our eyes on that bus."

The woman driving the van was humming along to the music on the radio, completely unaware that she was giving a ride to two dead dogs and a dead cat. It was probably better that way.

Patsy jumped into the front seat and put her paws up on the dashboard. After a few minutes, she called out.

"Uh . . . the bus is turning. Better hope we do, too."

"What if we don't?"

Patsy looked back at them.

"That's where the 'hopping' part comes in."

Brodie looked out the window. He could see the bus, heading off in another direction ahead of them. They waited as the van approached the intersection where the bus had turned.

"We're not slowing down!" Brodie said nervously.

"Get ready to jump," Patsy said.

"Where?" Tuck said.

"*Out*, idiot. We need a new ride. Ready?"

"No! I just got in here! And I'm not, like, super good at this!"

"It'll be all right, Tuck," Brodie reassured him. "Jump through the door just like you just did." He looked right into Tuck's eyes without blinking. "I know you can do this, man. Come on."

"Ready, guys?"

"Ready!" Brodie answered. Tuck remained noticeably quiet.

"Almost there. Remember we're moving. Hit the ground running."

"Right."

Tuck and Brodie stood side by side on the backseat, ready to spring.

"Now!" Patsy shouted.

A moment later, they were all running together on the sidewalk.

"Nice, Tuck! I knew you had it in you!"

"Thanks, buddy! I think I—"

"All right, all right," Patsy interrupted. "You can have a party later. Right now it's time to catch our next ride. Let's go with that one. The big yellow station wagon."

"But it's moving!" Tuck objected.

"Nice catch, brainiac. It don't matter. Here we go."

The cat sped up to catch the car, which was still moving slow after taking the corner. Without a look back she jumped easily through the door into the front seat.

"No fear, Tuck. Come on!"

Brodie charged forward and then bounded through the back door, coming to rest in the car's backseat. Before he could stand up and check on Tuck, the big black dog landed beside him.

"Nice, man!"

Tuck panted happily.

"I think I'm getting the hang of this."

They had to switch cars three more times to keep up with the bus. By their third hop, Tuck was leading the way, picking a car and jumping in without even waiting for Patsy and Brodie.

The last car was Brodie's favorite.

He didn't care that it had soft leather seats and a clean floor. He didn't care that the driver was listening to nice piano music on the radio. He didn't even notice, actually.

But there was a kid in the car. She was in the backseat. Reading a book. She had a backpack on the seat next to her. Sure, she was a girl. And, yeah, she was probably a year or two younger than Aiden was.

But still.

Her eyes were sleepy and puffy, like he remembered Aiden's had been in the morning.

Her pants were just a little too short for her growing legs just like most of Aiden's were, showing the brown skin of her ankle and the white of her sock.

As she read she smiled softly to herself from time to time, or pursed her lips, or raised her eyebrows at what was happening in the story. Just like Aiden did.

Brodie sat in the other backseat. Just looking at her.

Tuck and Patsy were in the front seat, watching the bus and arguing over whether they should upgrade to a car with a cleaner windshield. But Brodie ignored them. He just sat in the backseat, watching the girl's face as she read, watching the way she brushed her curly black hair out of her eyes, or rubbed at her nose, or sighed at the words on the page. Just watching the *kidness* of her. Just looking for little echoes of the boy he was seeking.

Because Brodie? That dog *loved*. He just loved. A lot.

Finally, though, his watching was broken by Tuck's voice.

"The bus is stopping, buddy! Behind a bunch of other buses!"

Their car was slowing, too, pulling over to the side of the road.

The girl folded down the corner of the page she was reading and slid the book into her backpack, then zipped it closed.

Tuck looked out the window.

He saw the brick building. The flagpole. The double front door. The stream of shouting, chattering kids walking inside.

"Hop out," he said. "We're here."

CHAPTER ELEVEN

"There's no use going in, you know." Patsy was sitting next to the sidewalk, out of the way of the last few kids still straggling into the building.

"What are you talking about?" Brodie asked, pacing back and forth.

"This is a huge school," she said. "Look at it."

And it was. The main building was three stories tall, and there were at least four smaller buildings around it. This had been Aiden's first year going to this school—*middle school*, Brodie remembered him saying—and it was way bigger than the school he'd gone to before.

"Hundreds of kids in there," Patsy went on. "Over a thousand, probably." The new words—*hundreds, thousand*—sprang into meaning in Brodie's head and he understood them. And he understood the truth in them. "You could walk around all day and never find him in there."

Brodie looked at the building full of countless kids, crowds of kids who were the *wrong* one, but that's not what he saw; what he saw was the *right* one, Aiden, somewhere in there, waiting to be found.

"You think I'm not gonna go find him, after all I went through to get here?" Brodie asked with raised fur, lifting his lip at Patsy and stepping toward the school.

Patsy yawned.

"Don't be so dramatic," she sniffed. "This ain't life or death, kibble-for-brains. You're already dead, remember? I'm just saying if you were *smart*, which you *ain't*, you'd just wait for—"

"I'm not waiting for anything," Brodie interrupted. "I'm going in. I'm finding my boy."

Brodie trotted forward, toward the double front doors of the school.

"Don't be an idiot!" Patsy called after him, but Brodie didn't slow down.

"All *right*!" Tuck exclaimed, jogging to catch up and run beside Brodie. "I *always* wanted to go inside a school! Hey . . . have you learned the word *cafeteria* yet, buddy?"

Brodie hadn't, but as soon as Tuck said the word, he got it. An image came together in his mind: a big room of long tables of kids. Kids eating food from trays. Food. Of course.

Brodie shook his head.

"Focus, Tuck," he said. "We're not here to find pizza crusts."

"Who said anything about pizza crusts?" Tuck asked. "I was hoping for something more along the lines of hot dogs. You ever had a hot dog?"

Brodie had. Despite himself, he licked his lips at the salty memory that surfaced in his mind.

"No," he lied. "And I need you to concentrate. You gotta help me find Aiden."

"Okay, okay," Tuck said. "What's he look like?"

"Uh . . ." Brodie thought about it. Aiden just looked like . . . *Aiden*. "Well, he's a boy."

"Yeah. I got that part."

"Short hair. Brownish. Like that kid's, but a little longer," Brodie said, gesturing with his nose at a boy walking in front of them. "About the same height as that girl with the skateboard, I think. And . . ." Brodie peered through the fog in his brain and looked closer at the most recent memory he had besides the monstrous one. He found the memory of throwing snowballs with him in the park, the happy memory filled with laughter and smiles, up until the end. "And he's got a blue coat. A big puffy one."

"All right," Tuck said, looking around. "Boy in blue coat. Got it."

The school doors closed in front of them. Through the doors, Brodie could hear a muted, echoey roar. It was hundreds of voices. Thousands of footsteps. Doors slamming, books dropping, shouted laughter, stamping boots. And, somewhere in that roar, one quiet boy who meant everything.

"Let's do it," Brodie said, and then he leapt through the doors with Tuck by his side.

What did they leap into? Absolute madness.

There were legs and feet everywhere. People screaming, yelling names, running and dancing and shoving. Backpacks being tossed, metal lockers crashing shut, snow-wet shoes squeaking on the muddy tile floor. More smells than you could wag your snout at, more sounds than ears could ever take in.

There was no way for Brodie and Tuck to dodge the kids, no room to stand off to the side. Kids passed through them, one after another, giving Brodie a shivery, rubbed-the-wrong-way feeling. He slunk to the side, spun, ducked, but it was no use. A parade of clueless kids walked right through Brodie's ghostly form, and each time it felt a little worse.

Even Tuck's wag lost some of its energy. He danced and darted, trying his best to find clear space to stand in—but he didn't find much, and what he found didn't last long. Some of the kids sort of shivered and stuttered when their living bodies touched Brodie's and Tuck's sparkling spirits, but most didn't even seem to notice.

"Let's go with the flow!" Brodie called. "Walk with them, it'll be easier!"

He slipped into the stream of traffic, sidling along between the clusters of kids, and it was better. He was able to slip between most of them without getting touched. He glanced back and saw Tuck doing the same thing behind him, walking between two girls tossing a basketball back and forth.

Brodie only made it a little ways down the hall, though, before his bubble of space collapsed and one, then two, then four kids waded blindly through him.

Up ahead, he saw a clear space. A little alcove off the main hallway, with windows looking out on the front lawn. "There, Tuck!" he called out, and surged forward through the crowd to reach it.

There was only just enough room to stand beneath the windows, but that's all they needed. Tuck scrambled to stand beside him, and they looked at the passing sea of rowdy kids.

"This is crazy," Tuck said.

"Yeah," Brodie admitted. "And . . . that *feeling,* when they walk through us. Why does it feel so bad?"

"It's your shine, idiot," a familiar voice drawled above them. Patsy's head was looking down at them. She was standing on the window ledge outside, with her head sticking through the window. "I tried to warn you."

"What do you mean, our shine? What's that have to do with anything?"

"It ain't just walking and sniffing and hellhounds that cost you shine, dogface. Anytime you touch the living—even though you can't really *touch* them—it wears your soul down. Every little brush, every little scrape. Every time one of these brats passes through you, you lose a little of your shine."

The cat tilted her head, looking at Brodie and Tuck.

"Yeah. You already lost some, both of you. You already got less than when you walked in here a minute ago." Her ear went back and her eyes narrowed. "All that beautiful shine, wasted."

"So, what do you think we should do?" Tuck asked.

"I already told you," she spat. "Quit wasting your time and your shine. Get the hell out of there."

"No way," Brodie said.

"Did you see him? Did you even really look?" Patsy demanded.

Brodie averted his eyes, dodging Patsy's drilling stare.

Because Brodie? The truth was, he'd forgotten to look. In all that craziness, in all the body-dodging and shine-losing, he'd forgotten to even try and find his boy.

But Brodie couldn't stand to admit that the cat was right.

"If you're not gonna help us," he snarled up at the scornful cat head, "then shut up. We're gonna go find him."

"Wait . . . hold on a sec!" Tuck said. A kid had stopped next to them to check something on his phone, and he'd set his backpack down on the floor. Tuck was sniffing the air . . . then he shoved his head through the fabric and into the backpack. His tail jumped into a high wag, and when he pulled his head back out, his eyes were sparkling. "This kid's got peanut butter and jelly!"

Patsy shot a withering look at Brodie.

"Well, if you got that genius helping you, what do you need me for?"

Brodie growled at her, and then turned and dashed back out into the hallway chaos.

He slid his way back into the stream of screaming kids, this time keeping his eyes up, scanning faces and looking for that one. He tried to sidestep, tried to slither and slip, but no matter what he did, he still felt hands, feet, legs pass through him. And each time, he felt the dip . . . the small but draining drip of his soul fading away.

He heard Tuck behind him, calling for him to slow down . . . but still he pressed on, his eyes always upward.

He saw smiling faces and worried faces, angry faces and hurried faces, brown faces and white faces and boy faces and girl faces . . . but he didn't see an Aiden face.

Borne along in the crowd of legs, Brodie passed another window alcove.

Patsy's flea-bitten face appeared again through a window.

"Stop being an idiot!" she hissed. "You're throwing your soul away for nothing! Do you ever wanna see that stupid kid again? Get over here!"

Brodie almost kept going . . . but then a whole group of kids, chasing and hollering, stampeded straight through him before he could get away. He felt it then . . . felt the excruciating tear of one of his shine lights ripping off and drifting away. Maybe even two.

Brodie whimpered, then growled, then darted with his tail between his legs to huddle under Patsy's head in the alcove.

When Tuck joined him, his ears were down, and even Brodie could see that the black dog had less shine than he'd had, less wag to his tail.

"This isn't working, buddy," Tuck said apologetically.

"No," Brodie admitted. "I don't think it is."

Brodie stood, looking hopelessly up at all the wrong faces passing by.

"Listen," Patsy said, and her voice had lost some of its nasty edge. "There's a hundred rooms in this school. By the time you get to the fifth one, you'll be lucky to have any shine left at all. Your soul will be gone, all that shine squandered, long before you ever find your kid. If you even do."

"So, what, you're saying I should give up?"

"No. I'm saying you should *wise* up. Every step you take, every breath of air you smell, every dumb kid that passes through you, you're losing soul. And for nothing. You know your kid's here, right?"

"Yeah."

"And you know he's walking out those front doors in a few hours, right?"

"Yeah."

"All right then, dummy. Why don't we sit out front and wait for him? He'll walk out, you'll be right there to find him, and you'll still have all your brainless soul to spare. It ain't that tough to figure out, even for a dog."

Brodie looked to Tuck.

"I hate to say it, buddy," Tuck said. "But I think the cat's right."

"Really?" Patsy asked. "Huh. Now I'm starting to doubt myself."

Brodie was just about to admit to Patsy that she was right when Tuck's breathless voice cut him off.

"Oh. My. God."

His whole body had gone stiff, and his eyes were locked wide, staring at something across the crowded corridor.

Brodie craned his neck, trying to see through the forest of legs to what Tuck was looking at.

"What? Do you see Aiden?"

Then the legs cleared for a moment, and he saw what had electrified the pit bull.

It was not a boy with brown hair and a blue coat.

It was a big room, with long tables, and kids eating food off plastic trays.

Tuck raised his snout, tasting the air.

"Do you smell that?" he asked, then turned intense eyes on Brodie. "It's bacon, buddy. *Bacon.* And . . . wait a minute . . . *oh.* Oh, man." The dog's eyes closed and his nostrils flared. "Pancakes. With syrup." He opened his eyes and looked back and forth between Brodie and Patsy. "You never told me they served breakfast at school."

"What?" Brodie asked. "Why would we—"

But it was too late. Tuck had already bolted, charging through the crowd to get to the cafeteria.

Brodie caught up to him just as he skidded to a stop inside.

"Tuck, seriously, we've gotta—"

"I know, I know. Just give me a minute, all right?" He stood, drinking in the air with his nose.

Brodie did a double take when Patsy scurried up beside them, her ear back and fur raised. Her head swiveled and her eyes darted, watching for oncoming feet.

"God, I hate kids," she growled.

"Then *you're* an idiot," Brodie said. "Kids are the best."

"Whatever. Let's get out of here. Save this moron's shine, and yours. And in a little while, we'll—"

Patsy's voice stopped short.

She was staring at a girl, sitting by herself at a table, sipping milk with a straw and reading a book.

"It's her," Patsy said, and her voice was the softest that Brodie had ever heard it. "It's her."

"It's who?" Brodie asked.

Patsy blinked a few times, then shook her head, looking away from the girl.

"No one," she said. "Let's go."

"Wait!" Tuck insisted. "You know that girl? Who is she?"

"I told you, she's no one."

But Tuck wasn't budging.

"Oh, she's someone," Tuck said, trotting toward the girl.

"Leave her alone," Patsy growled.

"What, was she your owner or something?"

Patsy's tail whipped angrily.

"I didn't have any *owner*. I ain't no pet. She was . . . just a kid I knew."

"You?" Tuck snorted. "I thought you were just a stray. How'd you know a girl?"

Patsy's body was still tight with anger, but her voice had a different edge to it. Or, really, no edge at all. When she spoke, her eyes weren't on Tuck or Brodie, but on the girl.

"Her family owns a restaurant downtown. They had one of the best dumpsters in town. Salmon skins. Chicken bones. Premium stuff. When they caught me eating, they'd shout and shoo me off. Like everybody else. But not her. She snuck me food, real food, in her pockets. She petted me. Talked to me. When I rubbed against her leg, she didn't kick me away."

Her eyes left the girl, and found Brodie's.

"She's the one that gave me the name Patsy. That's what she called me. She's the only person who ever called me anything. Well, the only one who called me anything *nice*."

They all looked at the girl for a moment.

She had thick glasses, and a purple turtleneck sweater. She was focused intently on the book in front of her, her lips moving soundlessly as she read.

All the other kids in the cafeteria were sitting in groups, laughing and talking with fast, loud voices. But Patsy's girl sat quietly, with only her book for company.

"Why is she all alone?" Tuck asked.

"Shut up," Patsy said. "There's nothing wrong with being alone."

"No, it's just that—"

At that moment, an empty milk carton flew from a crowd of kids at the next table. It bounced off the girl's tray and splattered the pages of her book. The other kids laughed; loud, mean guffaws. A kid with spiky black hair in the middle smirked and collected high fives from the boys around him.

Patsy's girl didn't look up. She didn't shoot them a dirty look, or roll her eyes, or call a teacher over.

She swallowed. Her face flushed red. She quietly, carefully used her sleeve to wipe the milk from her book. And she kept reading. But Brodie could see the wetness in her eyes. He could see the tears she was fighting back.

And Patsy? Patsy could see them, too.

"Let's get out of here," she said, turning back toward the hallway.

"What?" Tuck asked. "Don't you wanna—"

"No," Patsy spat. "I don't wanna."

And she left. She walked across the hallway, and out through the wall under the windows. And she didn't look back. Not once.

After a moment, Tuck and Brodie followed her.

So, outside . . . they settled in to wait.

Brodie sighed. The last bus pulled away. Only a couple of kids were still finding their way inside.

Remember the bigger truth, he thought. He'd found his boy. He knew where he was. What would he even do if he found him in there, anyway, in all that noise and crowd? And another part of his brain was whispering something else, too: *The danger is not at school. The danger—that shadowy monster—is at home.* He was so close, and he wanted to see his boy more than any words he ever learned could possibly express. But he hadn't just come back to see his boy . . . he'd come back to help him, if he could. To save him, if he needed to. And if it came to that, he knew he'd need some soul left to do it. If he went in there now, he'd be spending his soul for nothing.

Waiting was the smart thing to do.

Even though the smart thing to do? It's not always what the heart wants to do. Especially a strong heart.

But they waited. They crossed the street and waited under the tree that Brodie remembered, the tree that he had waited for his boy under, back when he had a beating heart and blood and breathing lungs.

Brodie settled in, there in the snow under the bare-branched winter tree. Patsy curled up on the hood of a car, parked against the curb. Tuck gave them both a look, almost started to sit down, then jogged off to investigate a cluster of garbage cans down the street.

Brodie had only a few memories of his boy. Only a handful had come back to him.

But, sitting there waiting for Aiden to come walking out the doors, they were all that he had. So Brodie closed his eyes and lived each memory, one by one, over and over, while he waited.

The park, the ball, the snow, the mud, the laughter, the hugs, the nights, the tears. Aiden standing atop the slide. Aiden's arms, tight around him. Aiden saying good-bye. Aiden hugging hello. Aiden's fingers, scratching at his fur. Aiden's eyes, looking into his own. Aiden's face, Aiden's smell, Aiden's voice, Aiden's smile.

Aiden's words: *You. Me. Together. Always.*

Time works different for souls without bodies. Without heartbeats or breaths to measure it, time can move in unexpected ways. For Brodie, waiting for the boy who meant everything to him, the hours of that school day could have and, yeah, maybe even *should* have felt endless. But Brodie, sitting there with his timeless memories, hardly noticed them pass at all. In his memories, he was with Aiden.

And being with Aiden? Well, Brodie would never get tired of that.

Tuck, though, was a different story.

The waiting was *way* tougher on Tuck.

Tuck circled. He barked at passing cars. He ran to the end of the road and back. He chased squirrels. He hunted fruitlessly for french fries.

"That dead dog," Patsy growled after a few hours, "is *not* resting in peace."

Brodie opened his eyes, shaking free of his memory to look at the cat.

"Yeah. I don't think he's the type," Brodie said. He watched as Tuck ran circles around an old man with a cane who was walking past. "Hey, how come we can pass through people so easily, without even trying? Our first night, before we met you, Tuck passed through some people, even before he knew he could. Shouldn't he have hit them like he hit that van door?"

"Nah. Stuff—trucks, vans, french fries—is easy. Living things are different. You can't touch the living, dog. We're separate from them, now. Forever. And I say good riddance."

Brodie looked closer at Patsy.

"Why? What's your story? You got a boy or someone you're trying to find?"

"I don't got no story, dog. I don't got no boy. Or no girl, not really." Patsy paused for a second, then lifted her lip in a quiet snarl. "I never had nobody. I just got me, and that's all I need. Got it?"

"All right, all right. I was just asking . . ."

"Well, quit asking. You should shut your mouth and start paying attention anyway."

"Paying attention to what?"

"The doors, genius. You wanna miss him?"

Brodie's head snapped back to the school.

Kids were filing out of the doors, laughing and talking back and forth. A bell rang, and the trickle of kids became a flood. A bus rumbled up the street.

Brodie jumped to his feet.

Tuck came running back to them from where he'd been trying desperately to chew on a cat who was dozing on a front porch.

"This is it," Brodie said, shaking with excitement.

"He's gonna come right by here, huh?" Patsy said, rising and stretching.

"You sure?" Tuck asked, sniffing at some bushes nearby.

"Yep. He'll be here." Brodie was sure of it. He'd watched his boy walk up this street countless times, and then walk back home the same way. He'd walked with him on the weekends, to play in the school's fields or shoot some baskets on the basketball hoops on the playground. This was the sidewalk he walked home on.

"Well, I hope he hurries," Patsy said in her bored voice. "And this kid better be something special, to go through all this."

"He is," Brodie said. "You'll see." He fixed his eyes on the stampede of kids pouring out the bright red front doors of the school.

They were bundled up in coats and hats and gloves, and their breath puffed in clouds in front of their faces. They shouted at one another and sang and laughed and chased. They paraded out, crazy and chaotic, stomping noisily onto buses or into waiting cars or onto sidewalks, heading home.

Tuck's tail was already wagging. Tuck was the kind of dog who couldn't help but wag when he saw kids, even when they weren't his.

"Where is he?" Tuck asked.

"I don't know."

"Is that him?"

"No."

"How about him?"

"Nope."

"Ooooh . . . there, running with the one glove! Is that him?"

"No, Tuck! Look, I'll tell you when I see him, okay?"

"All right, all right." Tuck trotted onto the sidewalk, wagging and sniffing at the kids as they passed.

Brodie scanned each face as they came out of the doors, looking eagerly from one to the next, waiting for the moment when he'd get to see his boy.

He saw big kids. Smaller kids. He saw kids with freckles on their cheeks and kids with metal shining in their mouths and kids with snot running down from their noses. He saw all kinds of kids, running happy out of that school into the cold air. But moments passed—long, waiting moments—and he didn't see the one kid he was looking for.

His stomach clenched and twisted.

His tail fell still.

The crowd of kids thinned out to scattered handfuls. Only a few kids were coming out now, in lonely ones and twos, running to catch up with the rest.

Tuck slowed his cavorting and playing. He snuck little glances at Brodie and then, after hours of constant motion, he stood still, his tail as limp as his friend's.

Two last kids went past them, both girls, heads held close together as they whispered excitedly in each other's ears. The last bus roared to life and rumbled out of the parking lot.

Tuck walked quietly over. He stood beside Brodie.

"He's not here," Brodie said. "He should be here. I know he should be here."

Tuck didn't answer.

Brodie stood, lost and shaking.

That memory echoed, the dark one, the bad one. The last one.

Brodie had left. But Aiden had stayed. He'd stayed there, with the monster lumbering toward him. With clenched fists, with deadly boots. With murderous eyes.

All of Brodie's soul was lost and scattered except for two questions:

Where was Aiden?

What had happened to his boy?

CHAPTER TWELVE

Brodie looked from the closed school doors to the backs of the last kids walking away down the sidewalk. He lowered himself to the ground and rested his chin on his paws.

"He should be here," he said again.

"Surprise, surprise," Patsy said from behind them. "This didn't end well. If only someone had warned you. Oh, wait. I did."

Tuck turned his head and lifted his lip at her.

"Shut it, hairball," he growled. "You're not helping." He turned back to Brodie. "Listen, buddy, just 'cause he wasn't here don't mean we won't find him. Maybe he, like, threw up or something. My girl did that once, and she got to stay home all day and watch TV. Her mom even let me lie up on the couch with her. We ate popcorn, man. *Popcorn.* You ever had popcorn? It's all salty and buttery and it sticks to your tongue and . . ."

"You're right," Brodie said, jumping up. "Aiden missed school all the time! He's probably just at home. He's *got* to be. Come on."

Brodie didn't have to think about the way home. He took off at a run, away from the school.

"You know the way?"

"Yeah, I know the way!"

Brodie led them at a run, down the street for several blocks before taking a couple of turns, first left and then right. They passed kids still walking home . . . Brodie and Patsy dodging side to side to slide around them, Tuck usually jumping rowdily right through them.

Brodie stopped for a minute at a corner to let Patsy catch up.

"We're close," he told Tuck. "We can cut down this alley." He spun in a circle, savoring the sudden familiarity of the street and houses around him. Memories rose into his mind in bunches now: chasing a cat into that yard across the road . . . finding a half-eaten hot dog in the vacant lot on the corner . . . ducking under that tree with Aiden during a rainstorm. He was home.

When Patsy finally trotted up—not in near as much of a rush as Brodie would have liked—they started down the narrow, unpaved alley. The snow was deep off the main streets. It would have come to Brodie's stomach in places, if they'd sunk into it. Walking on their ghostly paws, though, they stepped right along the top, leaving no footprints behind.

"It's right up there by the end," Brodie said, unable to stop the wag in his tail, "just past those kids playing around."

"They ain't playing around," Patsy said.

"What do you mean?" Brodie asked . . . but then he looked closer at the kids and heard the rawness of one boy's voice.

"Just go away!" There was a little anger in the voice . . . but it was mostly fear and tears and desperation. All of Brodie's wag withered away at the sound of it.

The boy was up on the roof of a low building—a *garage*, Brodie's mind told him—with his arms up over his face. Three bigger kids were on the ground beneath him. Two of them hurled snowballs up at his huddled body. These weren't the fun, soft snowballs of Brodie's happy memory with Aiden . . . they were packed tight and thrown viciously. They smacked the boy's upheld arms with hard thuds. The boys on the ground laughed. Their coughed-out laughs were as ugly as picked scabs.

Beside Brodie, Tuck whined softly. They both slowed, their eyes on the boys.

"Ugh. People are the worst," Patsy said, walking past them. "I'm glad I'm dead. These guys definitely look like the cat-torturing type."

Tuck and Brodie followed her, but more slowly. They both had their eyes on the jeering, shouting boys and the prey they had trapped.

Brodie stopped in the snow.

"I wish we could help him," Tuck said quietly.

"Yeah."

"Why?" Patsy spat, still walking on. "What'd he ever do for you? And, besides . . . you can't. Those guys ain't french fries. You can't touch *them*."

"It's funny," Tuck said, ignoring Patsy's words, "how different everything is now. How I can understand stuff. Back . . . *before*, if I'd walked past this, I probably wouldn't have even noticed how sad and scared that kid is. I'd have just seen the loud boys, heard their laughing. I'd have seen them throwing stuff and I would have wanted to play. With them. But now . . . now I can . . . *see* things better. Now *all* I can see is the sad kid, almost."

"I know. Me, too."

A gravel-speckled snowball rocketed up and glanced off the kid's huddled head, knocking his hat off. It slid down the roof and onto the ground.

Tuck took a step closer.

"I mean . . . I wouldn't have *cared*," he said. His voice sounded small. Sad. Ashamed, even.

But Tuck? He was wrong. He had *always* been the kind of soul who cared. And caring doesn't always need understanding.

"Well, you care now," Brodie said.

"Yeah. I do."

"Come *on*, fellas," Patsy called. She was well down the alley now, her tail whipping impatiently. "We got a different boy to find, right? And it ain't getting any lighter, either."

She was right. The winter sun was already low in the sky. Shadows from the trees and fence posts were stretching like black fingers across the white snow.

Brodie sighed. He tried to remember what the angel had said, tried to remember the *bigger truth*. But he couldn't tell, standing there watching the tears of the boy on the roof, whether the bigger truth would want him to find his own boy or help the one in front of him.

"Come on down and *play*," one of the trolls called. "Come on down, Danny, or we'll drag you down!" He started to climb up on a garbage can that was standing by the garage, probably the same one that Danny had used to get to the roof. The crying kid scooted farther up the roof. But there was no getting away.

"Come on," Brodie said at last, turning away. "We can't help him."

Tuck whined and shuffled his feet. But he turned and followed Brodie.

Behind them, the cries of the boy and the laughter of his attackers grew louder. The hunt was nearing its finish. Blood was in the water.

But then, Danny said it. He didn't shout it, or yell it. He said it.

"Leave me alone. *Please.*"

He didn't even say it like he was talking to the snarling monster who was climbing up toward him. He said it softly. Like he was saying it to the clouds. Like a prayer.

There's no way that Brodie should have heard it. He was down the alley a ways by then, and the boy said it so softly. But somehow the words got to his ear. Almost like they were carried by an angel.

Brodie stopped short.

He looked back over his shoulder.

It was the *please* that got him.

Because when that boy on that roof said those words, they echoed in a thousand woken memories in Brodie's heart. Memories of his boy. His boy had said those words, those exact words. He'd said them more than once.

Leave me alone. Please.

Brodie turned.

"Oh, just *don't*," Patsy moaned.

But Brodie did.

He ran back to the garage. Tuck ran beside him.

The goon was up on the garbage can now, one gloved hand holding the edge of the roof and the other swiping at the boy. Danny had his knees up tight to his chest. His pale face was wet with tears.

Brodie charged up and leapt at the boy on the garbage can with his teeth bared and a bark in his throat.

He flew right through the boy and landed in the snow on the other side.

He spun around and tried again. Again he ended up harmlessly on the ground, with the monster still standing on the garbage can.

"You *can't* touch the living!" Patsy called. "Have you listened to a word I've said?"

The creep stretched up on one foot and reached. His hand closed around Danny's pant leg. Danny cried out. But the creep caught hold and began to pull him down the roof. The boys waiting on the ground cheered.

Tuck tried, but he leapt straight through the kid just like Brodie had. He barked furiously, but Patsy and Brodie were the only ones who could hear him.

Brodie whined, his eyes on the crying boy. A boy he was helpless to save. It was all too familiar.

Dark memories swirled, choking him.

Then his eyes dropped down. To the garbage can that the monster was balancing on. It teetered and rocked as the monster tugged at his victim.

Tuck was barking and growling, running in circles and still jumping through the taunting boys.

"You can't touch them, idiot!" Patsy hissed again. "They're *alive*!"

But Brodie stepped forward, his eyes on the garbage can. *It* wasn't alive.

He remembered Tuck and the french fry. He remembered landing with a thud in the backseat when they were car-hopping.

He took off, running straight at the garbage can.

He focused on his shoulder. He concentrated his whole mind, his whole soul, on his left shoulder. He put everything he had into making that shoulder *real* and *solid*, like a dream come true.

He leapt. With his eyes closed and his every thought tightened down to nothing but that one shoulder, he leapt.

With a crash he smashed into the garbage can. He felt the frozen metal connect with his shoulder, and his body jerked to a stop. He opened his eyes in time to see the can tip and tumble onto its side.

The creep hung for a moment, one hand on the roof and the other clutching the boy. And then he fell, his body twisting as his hands slipped loose. He landed with a grunt and a smash on top of the garbage can. There was a brutal *thwock* as his face connected with the metal rim of the can. A splash of red blood splattered onto the snow. The boy rolled off onto the ground, groaning.

Brodie backed away from him.

The boy's friends stood back, their eyes wide.

"Dude, you okay?"

The boy moaned and sat up. Blood was smeared across his face and his nose was swollen and bent.

The boy wasn't a monster anymore at all. He was just a kid again, bleeding in the snow.

"Oh, dang!" one of the other boys said. "Your nose is totally broken."

The fallen monster didn't answer. His face was white, his eyes shining. He took a jagged, choking breath. A little moan started in his throat, but he grimaced and cut it off. Then he jumped up and stomped off, his hands over his nose. His friends hurried to follow him.

Brodie watched him go, unwagging. He knew what a hurt boy trying not to cry looked like. And he didn't like it.

He looked down at the blood, so bright and red and blaming.

On the roof above, the boy Danny was still sniffling.

But he was safe. Brodie told himself that. The boy was safe.

"Come on," Tuck said. "Let's go. He'll be all right now."

Brodie took one last look at the blood. Then he turned and joined Tuck and Patsy, walking away.

"You just blew *a lot* of soul, smart stuff," Patsy said. "And for what?"

"I helped him," Brodie said.

"Did you? So you think they're gonna be, like, best friends tomorrow? You think that creep's gonna be *less* mean tomorrow, *less* mad, when you've gone off to your precious Forever and the kid on the roof is still stuck down here? You think you *helped* him, mutt?"

"I did what I could," Brodie snarled, and he snapped at Patsy with his teeth. The fur on his back was raised and his lip was pulled back, showing the bright white anger of his teeth.

"Hey!" Patsy protested, flinching away.

"Take it easy, Brodie!" Tuck said, stepping between them.

"Yeah, psycho. I ain't got much shine left, you know, and I'm a helluva lot more interested in keeping it than you seem to be."

Brodie shook his head, flapping his ears and trying to clear the anger and guilt and hurt from his heart.

"Sorry," Brodie muttered, staring up ahead the way they were walking. "It's just . . . I didn't mean to *hurt* him, okay? But . . . but . . . I don't like it when big people are mean to little people. I don't like it when people are mean to *kids*."

"Sure, dog. I get it. But what *you* don't get is that none of this garbage is your problem. You don't belong in the world of the living anymore. All you're gonna do is make a mess. And lose your soul along the way."

"I did what I could," Brodie said again. "What else can we do? Yeah, I didn't fix the world. I can't fix that kid's tomorrow. Maybe all I can do is make today less dark for him. But if that's all I can do, shouldn't I do it?"

And Brodie? Brodie was right. That *is* all we can do. But that doesn't give us *less* reason to do it. It gives us more. Believe me.

And that kid, the kid up on the roof? He didn't know who to be grateful to. That's true. But he was grateful, all the same. He was.

And that other kid, the one dripping blood and anger onto the snow? Well, that kid's on his own journey, too. He's got his own darkness. And his own light. And pulling someone back from darkness, even if it's their own darkness, is always a good thing. It's always worth it.

The three spirits walked on, the shadows still growing around them.

"This is it," Brodie cut in, stopping abruptly. The other two stopped beside him. He was looking at the back of a run-down house with a falling-down fence and a glum yard strewn with junk. "This is it," he said again. His tail started to wag.

"This is our home."

CHAPTER THIRTEEN

Without even pausing to think, Brodie was running. He ran right through the gap-toothed fence—not even thinking as he leapt touchlessly through the wood. He raced through the dingy snow in the backyard, past the rusted-out wagon that Aiden used to play in, past the familiar red sled half-buried in snow, past the dented garbage can half-full of beer cans.

He stopped only once, and only for a moment. By the back door.

There were two plastic bowls on the porch. One red, one blue. Brodie remembered. Every day, Aiden had filled the red one with food and the blue one with water. For him. For Brodie.

They were still there. Empty, except for some snow, but there.

Brodie looked at them for just a moment, then ran through the back door and into his house.

When he was in, standing there in the dark little kitchen, he forgot Patsy's warning about smelling. He stood and sucked in one big, hungry breath. He let it tingle and swirl in his nose.

It was full of all the familiar smells of home. It smelled like food, and beer, and the old couch in the living room, and the shaggy stained carpeting, and the old coffee maker on the counter that was turned on every morning.

It smelled like Brodie, too . . . like his fur and his food and his wet, muddy paws.

It smelled like memories. Like nights curled up on the couch with Aiden, eating popcorn and watching the flickering lights of the TV. Like weekend breakfasts, and the strips of bacon that Aiden would slip to Brodie under that table.

But most of all, it smelled like Aiden. Like his breath and his body and his boyness. Like his hair and his clothes and his laugh and his eyes and the tight way that his arms hugged.

Brodie stood there, smelling and remembering and wagging. He stood there in his house and felt like he was at home.

Away. And Back. He was back.

But that wag? It didn't last for long. Because, little by little, Brodie realized he was not a lost dog, returning to his home. No. That's what he wanted to be. But he knew it wasn't the truth. Not anymore. Not ever again. That knowing rose up from deep down inside him, to front and center.

Because the Brodie smells—those doggy smells of fur and paw—were faint, and fading. They were already more like echoes than smells.

And on top of them were other smells he'd forgotten. Smells of *him*. Not Aiden. Someone else.

The shouter. The growler. The kicker and the hitter. The thrower. The drinker and the snorer.

Dad. The word was there. Aiden's *dad.* And with that word, all the blurry darkness of Brodie's worst memories came into focus.

That monster—the one who haunted his last memory, the one who snarled and charged and kicked and yelled and hurt—the monster who had called him back here, called him back here to save his boy? That monster had a face now, and a name. *Dad.*

It had a smell, too.

It smelled like beer and sweat and grease and piney aftershave and clothes worn too many times.

And that smell was all over the house, crowding out the smells of good memories and the smells of Brodie and even the smells of Aiden. *Especially* the smells of Aiden.

Brodie sniffed again, harder. Out of the corner of his eye he saw the bright glow of Tuck and the dimmer glow of Patsy step through the door behind him. But he focused on the smells of Aiden and how they smelled . . . stale. Faded. Old.

His tail fell still.

He didn't like what his nose was telling him. It was telling him that Aiden wasn't there. And that he hadn't been there in quite a while.

"No," he said. He ran out of the kitchen, down the hall, to the last room at the end. His memory was alive now, vivid and sharp, like he had just left—like he was still alive.

This was Aiden's room. The door was closed. The windowless hallway was dark. Brodie walked through the scratched-up old door and into Aiden's room.

If Brodie'd had a heart that still beat, it would have stopped. Not from fear. Not even from heartbreak. Just from *feeling.* Just from *too much.*

That small, messy, shadowy room was full to the ceiling with Aiden. With his smell. And his stuff. And his clothes and his bed and his backpack and his books. His pictures and his old toys and stuffed animals.

It was full of Aiden. So full of Aiden that if Brodie'd had lungs that still breathed, he would have been unable to.

But the room was also completely empty of Aiden.

The curtains were pulled closed. The bedsheets were thrown back messily like they always were, like he'd just gotten up. But Brodie could tell from the dormant dustiness of the room that Aiden hadn't been there that afternoon. Or that morning. Or even the night before.

His boy was gone.

Brodie walked over to the bed. He sniffed at the cold sheets, breathed in the smell of his boy. He knew that every smell cost him a little of his shine. But he didn't care.

"He's not here," Tuck said behind him. He didn't say it like a question, or even a statement. He said it like an "I'm sorry."

"No," Brodie said. His nose was still on Aiden's bed, the bed where he'd slept curled up with Aiden every night, the boy's arms snug and warm around him until he fell asleep and they went loose. The bed where they could be safe together. The bed where Brodie would lie, sometimes, and lick the salty tears from Aiden's face in the darkness.

"Is this him?" Tuck asked softly from beside Brodie. He was looking at a picture in a cheap fake-silver frame on the little table by the bed. Brodie knew the picture without looking at it. It showed Aiden kneeling down, his arm around a grinning Brodie. It was from the day two summers ago when they'd driven out to the lake. Aiden was shirtless and they were both wet and dripping, with water-plastered hair and wide summer smiles. Aiden was squinting into the sunlight.

"Yeah. That's him."

Brodie looked over at the picture. He couldn't talk for a minute, looking at those eyes and that face that he loved so much and missed so much.

"You'd love him, Tuck." Brodie stepped closer, lost in the picture and the memory. "He always sneaks me food under the table. And he's . . ." But then Brodie's words stopped short. Because he saw it, there in the picture, held in his boy's hand. Round. Yellow. The ball. That was it. The *Away*. And the *Back*.

All the memories came tied together, in one breathing, pulsing bunch.

Aiden, hurling the ball through the summertime park, cheering Brodie on as he sprinted after it.

Aiden, standing under a tree during a spring rain, laughing his Aiden laugh as Brodie slipped sloppily through the mud, bringing the ball back to him.

Aiden in the backyard, throwing the ball up onto the roof and cheering when Brodie leapt to catch it in the air when it rolled off.

Aiden, looking down at him with sparkling eyes and a ready smile, showing Brodie the ball, working him into spinning circles of excitement, desperate for the throw.

Aiden, sitting at one end of the hallway on a thunderstorm night, rolling the ball down the hall, sending Brodie into frantic scrambling to get the ball as it bounced between the walls.

Aiden, throwing the ball in sunlight and in shadow, in snow and under blue skies, across grass and mud and concrete and carpet.

Aiden.

And Brodie.

Brodie, running away. And back. Away. And Back.

This was their game. This was their rhythm.

Well. It *had* been their game. It *had* been their rhythm.

And now? Now they were stuck. Stuck in the worst place. *Away.*

And Brodie? Sure, he didn't have a heart that could beat anymore. But he still had one that could sing. And one that could break.

"Brodie?" Tuck asked, his voice gentle.

"He's bigger now," Brodie went on. "This is from a while ago." The picture was taken just after Aiden had lost a couple of his front teeth. Brodie looked at his big, gap-toothed grin. It was a smile that he loved. A smile that he hadn't seen much of for a while, even before he'd died. His boy, wherever he was, didn't do as much smiling as he used to. "He's taller now, and when we go for walks he . . ."

Again, Brodie lost his voice.

Because, once again and harder than ever, it hit him. He was looking at a dusty picture from a summer day years ago. A picture of a boy who was now different. And it wasn't a picture of a boy and his dog anymore. It was a picture of a boy and the dog he used to have. The dog who had left him.

"He looks like a fun kid, buddy."

Brodie couldn't tear his eyes off the picture, off that face and that smile and that arm around his body. It took a second for him to find the words, but when he did they were the truest thing he'd ever said.

"He's the best kid in the whole world."

Brodie sighed and dropped his head. He was going to rest his chin on the table, but it dropped right through the scratched wood.

He was dead. He was dead and his boy was gone. This was not his home anymore. This was not his *world* anymore. He was nothing but a dog in a picture. He was nothing but a memory.

"I don't want to be dead, Tuck," he said.

Tuck stepped closer to him, but didn't say anything.

"I don't want to be gone. I don't want to go to Forever."

"I know, buddy."

"I don't want to be anything but alive. And I don't want to be anywhere but here. With *him*." When Brodie had been alive, he'd seen Aiden cry. Plenty of times. He'd known that his boy was sad, and that had made *him* sad, but he hadn't gotten the crying. He hadn't understood how tears could come from eyes because a soul was sad. But standing there in that room with his boy gone and all the new words and understandings swirling inside him, he got it. If he'd had eyes that could cry, he would have.

"You did your best, buddy. You did everything you could. Don't worry. You'll be all right."

"I don't care about me, Tuck. I care about *him*. I don't want to leave him alone. I don't want to let him down. Not again."

"Not again?"

Brodie didn't say anything. He looked down at the carpet, breathing in the smell of his lost boy.

"Brodie? How did you die?"

Brodie looked up at him, looked into Tuck's warm and worried eyes.

Then he looked away.

"Okay," Tuck said after a moment. "Then let me tell you. Let me tell you how I died. Let me tell you why *I* won't go on to Forever."

"This oughta be good," Patsy muttered from the doorway. Brodie had almost forgotten she was even there. "Lemme guess. Choked on a hot dog?"

Tuck ignored her.

"I didn't have a boy. I had a girl. Emily. She was . . . just awesome, man. Just the greatest, you know? She ran with me. She fed me. She played with me. She named me Tuck but she called me 'buddy' when she was happy. And when she called me 'buddy,' man, I felt like the luckiest dog in the whole world. I loved her *so much.* You don't even know how much I loved her." Tuck paused. "Well, sorry. Maybe you do. But, man. That girl." He paused again, his eyes lost in memory. When he started talking again, his voice was softer. Hollow-sounding.

"But you know me. I . . . I get excited. I get distracted. And I love running. It's my most favorite thing. When I get the chance, when there's open ground in front of me and no leash around my neck, I just can't help myself. I forget everything else. I just *have* to stretch my legs and run, you know?

"It was morning. Emily went out to grab the newspaper off the front lawn. She left the door open. Just a crack. But it was enough. I nosed it open. I was just going to follow her. I swear. I was just following her. But once I got outside, I just . . . just lost it. The sun was shining. Birds were chirping. All those smells and sounds. You know how it is. I just . . . just *ran.* Right out of the yard, right down the sidewalk. Emily, she . . . she . . . chased me. She was yelling my name. I could hear it, hear her, I could hear the anger in her voice and then the fear. But I didn't stop. I wasn't running away from her, Brodie. I swear I wasn't. I was just . . . running. But she kept screaming my name. My girl, my Emily. She kept calling me. Telling me to stop. And I just kept going. I didn't listen to her. I didn't come back to her. I was a bad dog, Brodie. A bad dog."

Tuck's voice faded to a whisper.

"I didn't even see the car. I heard Emily scream. Oh, that scream. And then I heard a squeal. And then I was flying. And landing. And rolling. And bleeding. And *hurting*."

Brodie whined without even meaning to. He stepped closer to his friend.

"And then Emily came running up. And I was . . . I was . . . still alive. Hurting, bad, but alive. I couldn't move. And she was just crying and crying and petting me and crying. And people tried to pull her away and she wouldn't go. She wouldn't leave me. And all I could do was look at her. And I wanted so bad to stay, Brodie. So bad. I didn't want to leave her. But it was all going black. And I knew I was going. And I couldn't say good-bye. And I couldn't lick her hand one more time. And I couldn't say I was sorry. I couldn't say I was sorry.

"The last thing I saw was her looking down at me, crying and screaming. Because I ran. Because I didn't listen. She asked me to stay, she *begged* me to stay, and I ignored her. I abandoned her, Brodie." Tuck's last words came out shaky and ended rough. "I'll never be able to move on from that."

There was a silence.

"Why don't you go to her, then?" Brodie asked softly. "Why are you here with me?"

Tuck looked away.

"I . . . I couldn't. I couldn't look at her after what I did. What if she's still crying? Or what if she hates me? Or what if she . . . what if she has some new dog, some new buddy, who she loves more than me? Some dog who's good and doesn't run away? I couldn't handle that, Brodie. I'm not as brave as you are."

Tuck took a slow, long breath.

"But I figure . . . I figure if I can help you, if I can stick by you and help you do your thing, maybe I can, I don't know, make up for it. It's too late for me to be a good dog for her. But maybe I can be a good dog for you."

"Oh, Tuck," Brodie said, wishing that he could touch him, that he could nudge him with his nose and bump him with his shoulder and do all the things that living dogs do to say *I'm here* and *I'm your friend* and *We're together.*

"Oh, cry me a river." Patsy's voice broke the spell of Tuck's story. Both dogs turned to look at her. "You guys are *pathetic.* You really gonna spend all eternity whining about this? That you had these awesome lives with people who loved you and then you died? Well, guess what. *We all die.* And at least you had the first part."

Brodie took an angry step toward her.

"Why are you even here, Patsy? Really. If you don't wanna help, if you think we're so dumb and this whole thing is stupid, then why are you hanging around?"

"I told you, sausage-for-brains, I was bored."

"No way," Brodie snapped. "You wouldn't come all this way and go through all this stuff just 'cause you were bored. There's gotta be another reason. Tell us. What is it?"

Patsy looked at him, anger and uncertainty flashing in her eyes.

But she never got the chance to answer.

Because at that moment, a sound pierced the silence. It came from down the hall, from the front of the house.

It was the sound of the front door opening.

And then the sound of feet pounding inside.

CHAPTER FOURTEEN

Brodie didn't wait. He left Tuck behind, he ran right through Patsy (ignoring her hiss), and he sprinted down the hall.

Aiden! Aiden! Aiden! his heart sang.

He rounded the corner into the living room, his tail already in full wag, his bloodless heart bursting with joy.

But his paws stopped quick. And his tail stuck straight. And the hair on his back rose instantly into angry, ready spikes. And his lip pulled back so that the ghost of his teeth could shine white in the shadowy, cluttered room.

Because it wasn't Aiden's feet stomping in the door. And it wasn't Aiden standing in front of him.

It was *him*.

Big and burly and sour-faced. Shirt untucked, face unshaven.

Aiden's dad.

The monster.

He was there. And his fists were there. And his scuffed, rock-toed boots were there. And his glowering eyes were there. And his shouting mouth was there, shut silent but there in a tight angry line.

He slammed the door and sniffed loudly.

He looked right at Brodie.

And Brodie? Well, Brodie had years of practice with that monster. And when that man looked at him, Brodie cowered and backed away with his ears down and his tail tucked. It didn't matter that he was dead, didn't matter that the man's eyes and fists and feet would pass right through him without seeing or hurting him. Even ghosts can be scared of monsters, if they've been given enough reasons.

But the monster's eyes just slid past him, unfocused. He dropped a greasy brown paper bag on the coffee table in front of the couch and walked right *through* Brodie.

Brodie shuddered as the monster passed through him, too frozen with fear to move out of the way.

The monster shivered, too. He paused and cleared his throat, looked around for a second. Then he kept walking into the kitchen. There was the squeak of the fridge door, and the *click-pop* of a can being opened.

Brodie stepped out of his path as Aiden's dad walked back into the room and sat down on the couch, a can of beer in his hand. He turned on the TV and dug a hamburger out of the brown bag.

Brodie stood paralyzed, watching him. The monster chewed loudly, his mouth open. He already had a smear of ketchup on his chin.

Patsy and Tuck walked in from the hallway.

"Who's that guy?" Patsy asked, her voice low.

"I smell french fries," Tuck whispered.

"That's his dad," Brodie said. "Aiden's, I mean. He's . . . he's . . ."

There were too many memories choking Brodie's mind, too many pictures and sounds and feelings. And when he looked at Aiden's dad, the memories were all bad.

Bruises and bellows. Tempers and tears. Fists and fighting. Slaps and sobs.

And then it was right there. *The* memory. The one that had lurked and growled at the edges of his memory. The one that had haunted him and brought him back to this dark world with his soul glowing around him.

It was his last memory.

It had been nighttime. The sun had just gone down. Aiden and Brodie had been at the park, playing in the snow. They stayed as long as they could, like they always did. Aiden didn't like going home.

But, eventually, of course, they had to.

Aiden's dad had already been in an ugly mood before they'd left for the park. But when they got back, they'd known as soon as they'd walked in that it had only gotten worse. There was a pile of crinkled cans on the table. And he'd startled snarling even before the door had closed behind them.

It had been warmer that day. The snow had melted in places, leaving little muddy slush puddles here and there. Aiden hadn't really noticed. Until it was too late. Until his shoes and pants and coat were hopelessly muddy. Brodie, too, was matted and smeared with mud. They'd stepped inside, as quiet as they could. Aiden was hoping to get to his room, maybe, without the monster seeing.

But his dad was there, sitting on the couch, his eyes already narrow, red-rimmed and furious.

Aiden had stopped, right there in the middle of the carpet, his eyes wide.

Then the shouting had started, the yelling and cursing.

Aiden had apologized, like he always did. With his shaky and desperate voice. And Brodie had cowered, scared, but not leaving Aiden's side.

Aiden had gone back to the door and taken off his shoes, had wiped Brodie's paws. Then he walked with Brodie toward the hallway, either to get the vacuum or just to get away from his dad.

The monster had stood up, still snarling with his blurry voice and glaring eyes.

None of that was new. None of it was unexpected.

But then he'd thrown the can in his hand. Thrown it hard at Brodie. And it had bounced off Brodie's ribs. That was new.

It hadn't hurt that bad. Not really. It wasn't full. But Brodie had whined and flinched.

And, for the first time, Aiden stopped. He stopped still, and he stopped sudden. He turned and faced his dad. And he looked him right in the eye. And he talked back.

That was new.

"Stop it," he'd said, his voice soft but level and strong. "Leave my dog alone."

It took Brodie's breath away, that part of the memory. Alive, he hadn't known what the words had meant. He had only known that his boy had stopped and faced the monster. But now, remembering with all his new understanding and all his new words, he knew. He knew what his boy had said on that dark night to that roaring monster.

"Stop it. Leave my dog alone."

His boy, his brave and beautiful boy, had spoken for him.

"What did you say?" his dad had demanded.

And Aiden had said it again.

"Stop it. Don't you dare hurt my dog."

It was brave. It was beautiful.

And it was stupid.

The monster had roared and struck and the boy was on the ground before Brodie even knew what was happening. It was a savage strike. A hard, meaty fist, a vicious swing. A body-crumpling, blood-bruising strike.

Aiden had gone from brave and beautiful to broken and bloody in one breath.

His boy was hurt. He was crying. He crawled back into a corner, pulling Brodie with him.

But Brodie was shaking. His whole body, his whole soul, trembling in terror. He wanted to run. He wanted to get away.

And towering over them, a few steps away, with his hands in fists and his head rising and falling with his enraged breathing, was the monster.

Then: a mad, horrifying blur. Himself, shaking free and running away from Aiden. Aiden's screaming voice. Stomping boots. Beating fists. Broken bones. Pain. And then . . . separation. A leaving. Away.

It was all still a maddening mess, but through all the chaotic confusion one thing was clear and solid: the monster, with his raging eyes and snarling voice and thundering boots.

The monster.

Brodie stood there, right there in that same living room, and he looked at the monster on the couch.

"It's him," Brodie said. "He's the one. He's the one that killed me."

Tuck jumped forward, his fur instantly up and a growl in his throat.

"Easy, boy," Patsy drawled, although even she seemed to be eyeing the man with more than her usual hostility. "Dead, remember?"

"He . . . attacked us. Me and my boy. Shouting. Stomping. Kicking. Hitting. He was hitting my boy. And I . . . I was there with him." Brodie looked over to the corner, to the little area of dingy carpet next to the wall. That was where Aiden had been huddled. Where Brodie had cowered, paralyzed with fear. The rest of the memory was still lost in shadow, but he was sure that it ended there. That it *all* ended there, in that corner. That was where he'd died.

It was so shabby-looking. So . . . unremarkable. A stupid little patch of carpet. There was an empty straw wrapper against the wall. There was no sign of the terror. Of the fight. Of the end. Just a stupid little patch of carpet. There was nothing to show that that was where he was taken from his boy. And where his boy was taken from him.

And now he was here. And Aiden was gone. *Gone.*

A chill shivered Brodie's soul. He didn't know how the memory ended. He just knew that it ended here, and that it ended with the monster killing him. But what came after? Why was Aiden gone?

Brodie almost couldn't let himself think it. But there was also no stopping the thought.

What if Brodie wasn't the only one that the monster had killed that night?

What if Aiden was dead because Brodie hadn't protected him?

Brodie turned his eyes back to Aiden's dad.

Anger rose in him, hot and fast and unthinking.

He jumped forward and barked. He snarled and snapped and barked again, and kept barking.

The monster kept chewing, his dull eyes on the flickering screen of the TV. He took another swig from his can.

"Why did you do it?" Brodie shouted in his ghost voice, the voice that came from his head and his heart without sound. "Why did you do it?" He barked and howled and shouted out his anger at the man on the couch.

Tuck barked beside him, his teeth flashing and his muscles rippling.

Because Tuck? He was the kind of dog who stood by your side and showed his teeth to your enemies. Even if they couldn't see him. And a jet-black pit bull barking and snarling is a ferocious sight. Even if it's dead.

They stood there together, barking at the monster. They barked their anger and their fury at the monster and at all the other darkness in the world.

But, eventually, both dogs fell silent.

The monster burped and shoved a handful of fries in his mouth.

"Well," said Patsy behind them. "That was helpful. You gonna sing him a song now?"

Tuck shifted his paws, still glaring at Aiden's dad. He shook out his shoulders. He blinked. His tongue licked at his still-snarling lips.

"Man," he growled, "those fries look good."

"Where is he?" Brodie demanded, moving in front of the man's unseeing eyes. He'd stopped his senseless barking but he was no less furious. "Where is Aiden? Why isn't he here?"

The man sniffed and spat a loogie into the brown bag.

"Maybe he ran away," Tuck said. "Maybe they . . . took him away."

"Maybe he's dead," Patsy offered in her bored voice.

Brodie spun around.

"Don't say that!" he shouted. "Don't you ever say that!"

Patsy blinked.

"Fine. I won't *say* it. But I will say what I've been saying all along. You're wasting your time, pooch. Maybe he's here. Maybe he's gone. Maybe he's alive. Maybe he's . . ." Patsy paused, seeing Brodie's threatening step toward her. ". . . less than alive. My point is, it don't matter. *You're* dead. You can't do any good. You got nothing to do here, dog."

Brodie looked at her. He looked over his shoulder at Aiden's dad. He looked back to Patsy.

"I have to know. I have to know that he's okay."

"Yeah. You've mentioned that. Super exciting. Any leads on that?"

And it was at that moment, at that very moment, that the man's phone rang. The timing was . . . well, you could almost call it miraculous.

Brodie knew the ringtone. It was an obnoxious, whining guitar riff.

Aiden's dad swallowed his bite and washed it down with a gulp of beer while he fished the phone out of his pocket.

"Hello?"

Brodie sighed and looked down at the stained carpet. He couldn't see his next step. Everything he'd done had been to get here, to this house, to the place where his boy lived with the monster. And he was here and the monster was here and Aiden wasn't and it didn't make any sense and he had no more moves to make.

But his head shot up at the monster's next words.

"Yep, he's still gone." He said it low and seething. Angry. Brodie didn't care that he was angry. But he cared a whole lot about who the "he" was that Aiden's dad was talking about.

"Nah, they won't tell me where he is. 'Protective custody,' they say. Bunch of crap."

Those words meant nothing to Brodie but he took a step closer to the man, his eyes fixed on the man's mouth, begging him to say something that would lead him to where he wanted to go.

"Nope. Not even a phone call. Total bull. I mean, he's *my* boy."

Brodie's heart leapt. His tail almost wagged.

His boy was alive, and out there somewhere. Away from the monster. Safe, maybe.

"Yeah. Next week. Nah. I'll play nice for the judge."

Brodie waited breathlessly, sifting through the monster's words, looking for any clue.

"Yup. No kidding. All this trouble over that stupid dog."

Brodie's ears perked up. He must be the dog the man was talking about. Brodie started to growl, but the man's next words silenced him.

"Ah, don't worry. I will. I'll get my boy back. Yeah. See ya."

Brodie's half-excited wag stopped. The monster's words still hung in his head.

I'll get my boy back.

The man hung up the phone and went back to his food.

"Did you hear that?" Brodie asked.

"Yeah," Tuck answered. "He called you stupid."

"No, not that. My boy's okay. For now. But he's gonna get him back."

"What are you gonna do?" Tuck asked.

"Um, fellas?" Patsy cut in.

"I don't know," Brodie said, ignoring her. "But I gotta do something."

"Hey, guys? Hello?" Patsy said.

"How you gonna find him, though? I mean, if *this* guy doesn't even know where he is . . ."

"I don't know," Brodie repeated. "But I'll find a way."

"Hey!" Patsy shouted, stepping between them. "Quit ignoring me. You're being even more annoying than usual. Anyone else notice that the sun went down?"

"So?" Tuck asked. "You afraid of the dark, Patsy?"

"No, idiot. And neither are Darkly and his stooges."

Tuck and Brodie's eyes went to the window and the growing dark outside.

"Oh. Right."

"Quick, mutt," Patsy went on. "Feel him out. He coming?"

Brodie forced himself to take his mind off Aiden and the monster for a minute. He closed his eyes and felt through the dusk for Darkly.

There. He found him.

Brodie's eyes snapped open.

"Um," he said.

"Is he close?" Patsy asked.

"You could say that."

CHAPTER FIFTEEN

And then, right then, they heard the voices. Right outside the back door.

"You sure this is the place, boss?"

"Yeah, it's kind of a dump, Darkly."

"I'm sure, boys. He's around here somewhere. Check the garage, Thump."

"We gotta go!" Patsy hissed, heading for the front door.

"No!" Brodie protested. "I've gotta stay here and wait for Aiden."

"How dumb are you? You gonna just stay here and let Darkly rip your soul out? You gonna lose your soul in the same sorry place you lost your life, idiot? What good is that gonna do?"

Brodie paced anxiously. He eyed the monster, who was picking a piece of onion out of his teeth with his thumbnail.

"But . . ."

"Come on, buddy," Tuck said, his voice gentler than Patsy's but just as urgent. "We have to. We can come back tomorrow. Staying and getting torn up by Darkly isn't gonna help your boy at all. Let's go."

Brodie cast one last glance at the corner, that shabby little littered corner where he'd died. Then he snarled and followed Tuck and Patsy out the front door.

The last thing Brodie saw when he looked back over his

shoulder as he ran out of the room was Darkly's yellow face and black eyes coming into it.

"There they are! I've got 'em!" he howled.

Brodie jumped down the concrete stairs of the porch, right on Tuck's tail. Patsy was already on the sidewalk, sprinting down the street. Tuck and Brodie caught up to her under the light of a streetlamp.

The sky was dark, but not black yet. There was still a glowing line of blue and purple on the horizon. Snow was falling, big fluffy flakes, dropping down from the skies, fluttering through the gathering gloom to soften the dirty edges and lines of the city.

Behind them, Darkly and his three goons charged out of the house and onto the sidewalk, legs churning in hot pursuit.

"We'll car-hop," Patsy said, still running. "That's my trick, not theirs. We'll leave 'em behind, no problem."

A car was coming up behind them, heading the same direction they were going. It was moving quick. It was gonna be tough.

"You ready?"

"Ready," Brodie answered.

"Good. But I mostly meant the idiot. You gonna get this on your first try this time, smart stuff? 'Cause we don't got time for your stupidity."

Tuck didn't answer. He was eyeing the coming car over his shoulder, his mouth closed tight in concentration. The car was almost even with them. Tuck cut to the side and jumped.

He sailed right through the car's rear door. His head popped up in the window.

"Not bad," Patsy muttered, then jumped herself. Brodie leapt right behind her.

They both landed with a lurch in the car's backseat.

"That should lose 'em," Patsy said, hopping up onto the seat back to look out the rear window. "Those morons don't know how to car-hop."

Tuck and Brodie popped up, too, watching their pursuers.

Darkly and the others were running hard on the side-walk through the falling snow. A big black SUV pulled alongside them on the road. The hellhounds veered toward the street and, one after the other, hopped through the metal doors and into the SUV.

"Or maybe they do," Patsy said. "Huh. This could be a long night."

"What are we gonna do?" Tuck asked, his eyes on the car that was following them.

"We'll just have to keep hopping," Brodie said. "Stay ahead of them. Until sunrise."

"No," Patsy said, her voice low. "I can't do that. All these jumps, all this running and landing and hopping . . . it all takes a little soul, remember?" She looked down at her few remaining soul lights, circling slowly around her. "I don't got enough for all that. I'll be dark by morning. It'll be close even for you guys."

"Well . . . shoot . . . then . . . what *are* we gonna do?"

"Um . . . we're gonna get out of this car, to start," Brodie said. He was looking forward, out the front window.

"Why?" Tuck asked.

Right then, their car slowed to a stop at the red light that was glowing through the snow.

The black car pulled to a stop behind them.

Four hungry hellhounds piled out.

"That's why!" Brodie shouted, and all three of them leapt over the front seat and through the windshield and then scampered down the hood of the car. They jumped down onto the snowy blacktop.

The cross street was busier, and humming with traffic.

"That van!" Brodie called. They all saw the silver van coming their way from the left.

"But my shine!" Patsy called.

"I got ya," Tuck said, and leaned toward her with his mouth open.

"No way! Not ag . . ."

But Tuck snagged her kicking body in his jaws and bounded through the side of the van that was speeding past. Brodie was right beside him.

Patsy was already snarling and swiping by the time they landed inside. When Tuck let her go she was already in mid-shout.

"You listen to me, you stupid mutt. I swear I will rip your ugly . . ."

"Oh, zip it, Patsy," Tuck said, not even looking at her. His eyes were out the window, watching as the hellhounds hopped into a pickup truck a few cars behind theirs. "I know you don't like it but you're gonna have to deal. You got any better ideas for staying ahead of those guys *and* not losing your soul in the process?"

Patsy glared at him, her eyes flashing and her tail whipping furiously.

"I didn't think so," Tuck said. "So get used to it. It ain't a treat for me, either, you know. You ain't exactly a french fry."

"We got another light coming up!" Brodie announced.

They all stretched to look.

"See that yellow car coming the other way?"

"Yep."

"If we jump now and switch directions it might catch them off guard. We could put some distance between us."

"Got it. You give the signal. You ready, Patsy?" Tuck asked, bending toward her.

Her only answer was a growl. But she didn't slash with her claws or run away.

Tuck picked her up in his teeth.

"Now!" Brodie shouted.

They burst through the side of the braking van and landed with stumbling feet on the painted line between the lanes of the road.

The yellow car was already right there, speeding in the opposite direction. Without even a chance to get their feet properly under them, Brodie and Tuck sprang into it.

"That was close," Tuck said, spitting out Patsy on the backseat. "Did it work?"

Brodie had his nose against the back window.

"Kind of. They're still behind us, but now they're a few more cars back. In that red car with the dark windows."

"Well, at least we've got some time to figure out a plan," Tuck said.

"How you doing, Patsy?" Brodie asked.

The cat looked up. She'd been angrily licking at her back where Tuck had held her.

"This is the worst night of my life," she said. "And I'm not even alive."

"At least it's working. It looks like you've still got as much soul as you started with."

"I wish I could say the same for you guys," she said, looking at their shine. "That last hop especially cost you. The faster we're moving, the harder you hit, the more soul you lose."

"Well, we don't have a lot of choices."

"Uh-oh," Tuck interrupted.

"What?"

"Their car. It's moving faster than ours. It already passed two others."

Brodie joined him at the window. There were only two cars between them and the red one now. It was in the next lane over. As they watched, it pulled past another car.

"You're sure they're in it?" Tuck asked, squinting at the darkened windows of the red car.

"Yeah. I saw them hop in. This is bad."

They were really moving now, the street humming underneath them. Brodie looked through the front window. The traffic was moving smoothly ahead of them. There was no sign of a stoplight.

The red car passed the last one between them. It was coming up on their rear bumper now.

They passed under a streetlight, and Brodie could just make out the shapes of four dog heads in the front and back windows, pressed right against the doors.

"Oh, man," he said. "They're gonna jump."

"Why would they do that?" Tuck asked nervously. "They're gonna catch up to us."

"No," Brodie said. "Not jump *out*. Jump *across*. Into our car."

The red car was almost even with them now, right beside them in the other lane. The shadowy dog heads bobbed excitedly.

"Oh. Yeah. That makes more sense."

"We've gotta jump!"

"We're going way too fast!" Patsy warned. "You'll burn too much soul!"

"Again, Patsy," Brodie growled. "No choices!"

"I'm telling you, we're going too fast!"

"They're almost here!"

"We've gotta do it!"

Their shouts competed with the roar of the car engine and the rumble of the road beneath them. The headlights of passing cars and streetlights cast crazy shadows and glares around them.

"There's no way that you can—"

At that moment, Darkly's big golden body came ripping through the side of their car, his eyes blacker than the night sky and his teeth out and ready. The other hellhounds were right behind him.

There was no more time for argument or for waiting.

Brodie bared his teeth and jumped out through the other side.

He hit the snow-dusted sidewalk hard. His paws had no chance to catch him and he rolled, pinwheeling and tumbling along the concrete, the world a crazy spinning blur of headlights and dark sky and cold pavement.

He came to rest beside a fence—not hurt, but shaky and senseless.

A small whimper slipped out of his throat.

Because Brodie? He'd felt it. He had felt the chipping away of his soul with each thump and scrape. He had felt the wearing down of his spirit. The lights swirling around him were fewer, and more lonely. The world around him seemed a little more dark, a little more cold.

He shook his head. Tuck was sitting a little ways away from him, also shaking his head but already rising to his feet.

"That *sucked*, buddy," he said.

"Yeah," Brodie said. He looked around. "Hey. Where's Patsy? Didn't you grab her?"

Tuck's tail went down.

"Oops."

CHAPTER SIXTEEN

"Come on!" Tuck said, taking off after the speeding car they'd just jumped out of. Brodie followed without thinking.

In no time Tuck was well ahead. Brodie was no match for his full-on, from-the-heart strides.

He looked to the side.

"White car!" he shouted ahead, hoping Tuck could hear him. "I'm hopping in!"

Brodie put everything he had into his legs, squeezing as much speed out of them as he could. The car pulled up beside him and he jumped, passing through the front door and the front seat before landing abruptly in the backseat next to a kid with his eyes glued to a video game in his hands.

He straddled the kid, looking out the window at Tuck running on the sidewalk.

Tuck looked back, but it was too late. The car was already going past him. He turned on a surge of speed and jumped.

Brodie stepped back to make room, but Tuck's timing had been off.

His head popped into the car for just a second, his eyes wide and tongue flopping, but it disappeared through the backseat as the car raced forward.

There was a thump from the back of the car.

"Tuck!" Brodie screamed, jumping up to look desperately out the back window.

The road behind was empty, though, except for snow and other cars. There was no sign of Tuck.

"Yeah?" Tuck's voice answered.

"Tuck? Where are you?"

"Uh. Someplace dark. And loud. The trunk, I think."

Tuck's head appeared through the backseat.

"Yep. I was in the trunk." He jumped into the backseat and then straight on into the front of the car, straining to see out the windshield.

"There it is! I see her!"

Brodie joined him. Two cars ahead of them was the red car. Patsy was up against the rear window, on the ledge behind the backseats. She was twisting and dodging and swiping with her claws. Brodie could see dog tails and heads jumping and spinning and rising and falling in the seat in front of her.

It looked like quite a fight.

"If we get to a red light, we can go save her!" Tuck said, his voice tight.

Brodie didn't say anything.

"But we should have a plan! Any ideas?" Tuck asked.

Brodie was still silent.

"Buddy? Any idea for a plan?" Tuck looked at him.

Brodie's ears drooped.

Because Brodie? Brodie was a good dog. And sometimes good is a tough thing to be.

"What?" Tuck asked.

"Listen, Tuck. This is our chance."

"Our chance to what?"

Brodie looked away. Out the window. Away from that mangy cat, trapped and cornered and fighting for her soul. Away from the purehearted dog beside him.

"They're . . . they're distracted, Tuck. And they're speeding *away* from us."

Tuck's mouth closed.

"What are you saying, buddy?"

Brodie didn't want to. He didn't want to say it. But he had to.

"You know what I'm saying. I think we should go. While we can. Get away."

"What, and . . . leave Patsy?"

"This is our chance," Brodie repeated.

"But she needs us."

"I . . . I need to get to my boy. I can't waste any soul on her."

"Waste? But . . . Patsy's our friend."

Brodie looked away again, out into the darkness.

"Barely. Come on, Tuck. Let's go while we can."

Tuck looked at Brodie for a long, wordless moment. Brodie couldn't meet his eyes. Finally, Tuck spoke.

"Okay, buddy. Okay."

Brodie's tail almost started to wag. But then Tuck kept on talking.

"You go ahead. I'm not gonna leave Patsy. Not like this. I'll . . . find you later. I'll meet you back at your boy's house. If I can."

Tuck looked away, back toward where Patsy still swirled and struck at the hellhounds surrounding her.

Brodie wanted to say something. He wanted to argue. But no words came. There was nothing to say. He had to get to Aiden. He had to. So he had to leave those hellhounds behind. And this was his best—maybe his only—chance. But he could tell from Tuck's eyes, from his voice, that that dog wasn't ever gonna leave that cat to get torn up by those hellhounds.

Brodie turned to the door. He looked out at the snow-speckled night. He eyed the sidewalk, which was a blurry obstacle course of garbage cans and parked cars and light poles. He needed a clear place to land. It wouldn't hurt to crash into anything, he knew. But he didn't want to waste the shine.

Up ahead, he saw it. A nice stretch of clear pavement.

He looked back at Tuck, who still stood with his eyes on Patsy's struggle. That dog was ready to do battle. His eyes were ready. His muscles. His teeth. His heart.

"Be careful, Tuck."

Tuck looked at him, once, then away quickly.

"You too, buddy."

Brodie turned back to the window. They were almost to the jumping place. He readied his legs for the leap. His soul swirled around him.

And then the memory came. It rose like a sunrise, all glow and shine, but fast. It was from that day. The one in the picture by Aiden's bed.

Sunlight dancing on water. The sweet smells of summer mud and soda pop and soggy swimming suits.

They were at a lake. It was a good day. The monster was there but he wasn't growling or snarling or drinking or shouting. He was just talking. Laughing sometimes, even. Aiden was happy. It was a good day.

Aiden was throwing the ball. He was throwing it off the end of a long wooden dock that stuck out past the tall weeds around the lake's edge. And Brodie was running, claws clattering on the dock planks, and then he was jumping and then soaring and then splashing and then swimming, paddling through the water after the yellow bobbing ball. Swimming, Away. And Back. Clambering back up onto the dock, dropping the ball at his boy's bare muddy-toed feet, and then shaking the water off his body. Aiden was laughing, giggling, breathless. Beautiful.

Brodie, panting, had flopped down onto the wet wood to rest. Aiden had sat down beside him, legs dangling over the dock's edge, toes splashing in the water. He'd wrapped a skinny, goose-bumped arm around Brodie's shoulders and Brodie had looked up into his sun-silvered eyes and he'd almost stopped breathing he was so in love with that boy.

"What a dog," Aiden had said with a smile, shaking his head, and his wet hair had flopped down into his eyes. He'd leaned in close with his Popsicle breath and whispered again those four words: "You. Me. Together. Always." He'd scratched at Brodie's wet head. "Right, Brodie?" And then he'd laughed his perfect Aiden laugh. Just because it was a good day. Just

because they were there together. "Man," he had said, shaking his head again and looking deep into Brodie's eyes. "What did I ever do to deserve a dog as good as you?"

That. That was what he was fighting for. That's what he would brave heaven and hell and everything in between for. That's why he would leave Tuck and leave Patsy and face the dark world alone. That boy. That love. That *Always.*

He braced his paws, bunched his muscles. He would land running, sprint back the way they'd come, while the hellhounds roared off in the opposite direction. He'd never see the hellhounds again.

Or Patsy.

His opening came. The empty, waiting sidewalk. It zoomed closer and closer, and then it was right there right in front of him—and then it was gone, receding into the distance as the car sped away. With Brodie still in it.

He closed his eyes, felt the humming of the car, remembered the golden glow of his boy's face on that sunny summer day. He'd been ready to jump. He had been.

And then his boy's words had whispered again in his head.

What did I ever do to deserve a dog as good as you.

And then the words of an angel-who-wasn't-an-angel.

You're good dogs. Remember that. Be good dogs.

Tuck had remembered. Brodie, for a while, had almost forgotten.

He didn't have to abandon Tuck and Patsy for his boy.

No.

He had to stay and stand with them. For his boy.

His boy loved him, with all of his heart. It was a big love. And he had to be worth it.

That's what love does, I guess. It makes us bigger.

He turned to face the front, standing shoulder to shoulder with Tuck.

Tuck looked at him.

"Aren't you going?"

"No. I'm staying. With you."

Tuck's stubby tail went back to wagging.

"What about your boy?"

"I'll find him. I will. But my boy . . . he . . . he deserves the best dog in the world. So that's what I gotta try to be."

Tuck's tail whipped into double time. He grinned wide and toothy at Brodie for a minute, then looked back out the windshield at that cat, still swiping and slashing and swinging in the car ahead.

"Thanks, Tuck," Brodie said after a while.

Tuck looked at him sideways.

"For what?"

"For being a good dog. Now let's go save that mangy cat."

Tuck's tail jumped into full puppy wag.

"Yeah! Let's do it, buddy! You got a plan?"

"My plan was to ditch her. What's yours, hero?"

But there was no need for a plan. Because right then the windshield was lit up red by the brake lights of Patsy's car in front of them. Their own car started to slow.

"It's go time," Brodie said. "You ready to grab her?"

"Oh, yeah."

"All right. That's our plan, then."

They jumped from the car before it stopped moving. Patsy did the same, a moment after them.

She hit the sidewalk sideways with her back to them and before she even took a step, Tuck scooped her up and they were off, sprinting down the sidewalk with the hellhounds on their trail.

For once, Patsy didn't complain about being in Tuck's mouth, even though she was bouncing and swinging and jostling as Tuck pumped his legs furiously, trying to put some ground between them and the hellhounds that howled and snarled behind them.

"You idiots came back," she said.

"Of course we did," Tuck said, and he didn't even hesitate or shoot a dirty look at Brodie when he said it.

Because Tuck? He was the kind of soul who saw the best in others, and didn't waste time on the worst.

Brodie eyed Patsy as they ran.

"Your soul," he said.

"What about it?" she snarled, dangling from the pit bull's jaws.

"It's . . . almost gone."

Patsy only had a few lonely little soul lights left, faint and wispy.

"Yeah, so what?"

"They took some, didn't they?"

Patsy spat.

"You kidding? I'd never let those black-eyed mutts get a bit of *my* shine. These claws are sharp enough to keep a few brainless ghosts away. It's all this car-hopping and running. I didn't have much to start with, and I've been spending it fast with you two idiots."

Brodie looked back. As usual, the hellhounds couldn't keep up with their pace on foot. But they weren't going anywhere.

"So what's the plan?" Patsy asked.

"You're looking at it," Brodie said.

"What, run till sunrise? That's your plan?"

"You got a better idea?"

The snow was falling harder now, fluffy white flakes tumbling all around them. The sky was dark and cloud-choked, the sun gone for good. It was nighttime, and the hellhounds were following close, and their own souls were twinkling out, light by light.

Brodie's mind raced as he ran, looking for a way out. Looking for a way to leave the hellhounds behind so he could find his boy, his Aiden. He searched in the darkness for an answer . . . and found nothing.

But then Tuck spoke.

"I've got an idea."

"Oh, yippee," Patsy said. "Does it involve bacon?"

"Come on."

Tuck cut sharp into an alleyway. It was dark and shadowy. The snow, untrammeled by cars or feet, was a soft blanket on the ground.

Halfway down the alley was a dumpster.

Without a warning, Tuck jerked his head and tossed Patsy up into the air. She somersaulted in flight, hissing and spread-legged, before landing gracelessly on the dumpster.

"What in the world—" she started to shout, but Tuck wasn't listening.

"Now you," Tuck said, stopping beside the dumpster and looking at Brodie.

"What?"

"Get up there," he said. "Jump off my back to the top."

"What about—"

"Go! Now! Trust me!"

Brodie hesitated a moment, then backed up a few steps. He ran and sprang, leaping with his feet off Tuck's waiting back. His front paws made it on top of the dumpster and he scraped with his back claws, finally helped up and over the edge by a shove from Tuck's stretching nose. He spun around.

"What about you? How are you getting up?"

"I'm not."

"What?"

Tuck looked up into Brodie's eyes. His face was serious. Grim. But calm.

"It's the only way, buddy. They can follow us forever as long as Darkly's got your soul. So I'm taking it back."

"Tuck, you can't! How will—"

"Listen," Tuck said. His voice was quiet. Firm. His words came fast, but they rang with the sure strength of a soul speaking its truth. "I'm doing this. I'm doing this for you. I'm doing this for your boy. And I'm doing it for my girl, too. I'm doing it for Emily. I'm not running away this time, Brodie."

"There they are!"

Darkly's voice roared down the alley. The four hellhounds came galloping down through the shadows toward them.

"Time's up," Tuck said, turning to face them. "Listen, buddy. Just watch Darkly's shine. When it's gone, *run*."

"Tuck, this is crazy! How can you—"

But Brodie was stopped by Patsy's voice, low in his ear.

"Shut up," she said, quiet.

"What do you mean?"

"The idiot's right. It's the only way. Let him do it."

Brodie snapped his head to look at her.

"That's easy for you to say! You hate him!"

Patsy gave Brodie a long, unreadable look. She blinked. Then she looked away.

"It's the only way," she said again. "Just be ready to run."

Tuck stepped forward, toward the coming danger.

The swirling lights of what was left of his soul cast a shimmering glow on the brick walls surrounding him and the pure snow under his paws.

He didn't whimper. His head was high. He didn't run. He didn't tremble.

Because Tuck? Tuck was Tuck. And Tuck was . . . well, he was really something.

The dogs stopped several paces away, black eyes glittering suspiciously.

"What's your game?" Darkly asked.

"No games," Tuck answered, his body tight and still. "Just teeth. But they're all yours, Darkly."

Darkly's golden tail wagged. The stolen soul lights danced around him, sparkling against his yellow fur. He was down to only two.

"You know you can't win, right?" he asked. "We can't die. You can't beat us."

"We'll see."

"Yeah," Darkly said, edging in closer with his cronies. "We'll see, all right."

Tuck stood between the demons and his friends. The hellhounds stood in a tight circle, walling him in. The alley below the dumpster was all black eyes and bared teeth and one brave, shining soul. The air crackled.

"Don't worry about taking turns, boys," Darkly growled. "We can do that with the other one. This tough guy? Just dig in. Let's shred him."

There was no moment of waiting. No breathless second of anticipation. At Darkly's words, the battle began.

CHAPTER SEVENTEEN

It was quite a fight, that final fight when Tuck offered up his own soul to save Brodie's. Quite a fight, from quite a dog.

There was a lunging of bodies. A baring of teeth. Throats full of snarls. And the fight was on. A swirling, swarming, surging battle that would have quickened the pulse and chilled the blood of anyone who watched, alive or dead. Even an angel might have gone pale at the ferocity of it. Believe me.

And Tuck? Tuck was a warrior. He was all muscle, all tooth, all heart. He was every inch and ounce a fighter. Especially when he was fighting for something.

But Tuck? Tuck was one dog. One dog, surrounded by four soul-hungry killers.

He never stopped moving, that Tuck. He spun and he slashed and he snapped and he stood his ground.

They flew at him, lips pulled back in ugly hunger grins. One at a time or two by two or all at once. They darted and dodged and roared and retreated and came back again, fangs first. And he fought them. With all the heart of a hero.

But he was one. And they were many.

Brodie saw it. The moment that Tuck first lost a piece of his soul.

He'd fought two of them away, forced them back with yips of pain from his brave bite . . . but then Smoker slipped to his unguarded flank and, before he could turn, sank his teeth deep into Tuck's black body.

Tuck spun but Smoker held tight. He shook his head, tearing and chewing at Tuck, and as Brodie watched, one glowing light, and then another, tore free from Tuck and then circled slowly around Smoker.

Tuck whimpered, a high desperate whine, and then raised his head to the blackness of the sky and howled. It was a howl of loss, of pain, of agony. Brodie knew that sound, knew the feeling of having your soul torn away. Watching from above, what was left of his broken heart cracked a bit more at the horrible howl of his friend. He stepped to the edge of the dumpster and readied his paws for the jump. But he felt Patsy's claws sharp on his shoulder.

"No, idiot," she hissed. "Don't. This is his to do. Let him do it."

Below them, Tuck ended his howl with a snarl and swung his body viciously, tearing Smoker free and tossing him tumbling into Skully and Thump. They fell in a tangled pile against the far wall. And without a breath, Tuck leapt at Darkly.

Darkly was ready for an attack. But he wasn't quite ready for a Tuck.

He blocked Tuck's first strike with his own teeth but faster than fire, Tuck struck again and then again, high and then low and then right down the middle and then turning and diving. Darkly blocked and dodged but he didn't have Tuck's speed or Tuck's heart.

Tuck got through and his teeth found yellow fur and they sank deep and held.

The other hellhounds, back on their feet and ready to rumble, tore into Tuck's haunches.

The whole pack, Tuck included, held together by tooth and jaw, circled and stumbled.

Tuck's high whine pierced the noise as two, three, four, five of his soul lights were ripped from him. But his grip never wavered, and one of Darkly's two lights began to tear free and drift toward Tuck. And then it was Darkly's turn to howl.

Darkly's pain came as a roar and he twisted wildly, tearing free from Tuck's teeth just in time . . . the soul light he'd almost lost, the one that Tuck had nearly stolen back, stayed with the horrible hellhound. Tuck rolled and spun and shook the hellhounds off.

There was a breath, a hard-as-metal sliver of time when all the fighters stood facing one another in the darkness, their eyes fierce and their teeth bared. But only a breath. And then with murderous growls they leapt into the final battle.

Tuck charged for Darkly but the hellhounds got to him first, finding his shoulders, his back, his flank with their teeth. Tuck slowed but did not stop as they tore at him. Darkly stepped back as Tuck struggled forward, dragging the demon dogs with him.

"That's it, mutt," Darkly growled, backing slowly away as Tuck advanced. "Let us have it all."

A high, tortured whine scraped from Tuck's throat with every step. His soul lights, one by one and two by two, ripped away from him and flew to his attackers.

He slowed with each step. That dog, that brave dog, had taken on too much. There is a limit to how much any one soul can do, no matter its courage or worth.

With a groan and a whimper, Tuck collapsed to the ground. The hellhounds dug their teeth in deeper. Their terrible tails wagged as they feasted on his soul.

If any angels had been watching, they surely would have nearly wept. Surely.

Darkly stepped forward to stand over Tuck, defeated.

"All that foolish fighting," he sneered down into Tuck's desperate, begging eyes. "It only makes your soul all the sweeter."

The other hellhounds still tore at Tuck, tearing away his shine drop by drop.

He had only five lights left. Then four.

Brodie bunched his shoulders to jump.

"Don't," Patsy whispered to Brodie. She'd seen him, ready to leap down, ready to lose his soul by Tuck's side.

Three lights left.

"Look at his legs," Patsy hissed.

Brodie squinted and saw.

As Darkly gloated over him and the hellhounds tore his soul away bite by bite, Tuck gathered his legs slowly up underneath himself. His hind legs were springs, taut and ready. His front claws dug for footing in the alley gravel.

And his eyes, if you knew how to look, were not begging. They were waiting.

But his shine was down to almost nothing. He was almost dark.

But almost? Almost doesn't mean a thing for a soul like Tuck's. He was almost dark, but believe me . . . he was nowhere near surrender.

Two left. Then one of them broke free and circled around Smoker's greedy, chewing jaws.

Tuck had one light left. One glowing shine.

"Slow down, boys," Darkly said, licking his hungry teeth. "I get the last bite." He took one last step closer so that he was only inches away. "Are you ready to lose your soul, dog?"

Tuck answered, but not with a word. He answered with a roar and a lunge.

His legs rocketed him forward, tearing him free of the hellhounds and hurtling him teeth first into Darkly's throat. His jaws closed and held.

Darkly choked out a strangled cry of fury, of surprise, of pain. And then of loss.

One soul light—stolen from Brodie, and now stolen back—broke free and flew to the pit bull at his throat. Then, as Tuck dug his teeth in deeper and yanked with all his heroic rippling strength, the other light followed, leaving Darkly to swirl around Tuck.

Darkly howled like all the light, all the joy, all the hope, had been ripped away from him. Because it had been. Believe me, it was a terrible sound. It was the kind of sound that made you wish you could close your ears like you can close your eyes. It was a sound that raised all the fur on Brodie's back.

The other hellhounds stepped back uncertainly.

"Go!" Tuck shouted without letting go. "Go, Brodie!"

Brodie whined atop the dumpster, his eyes on his fearless friend.

"Now, idiot," Patsy hissed. "If you don't go, it was all for nothing."

She sprang down to the ground and sprinted away up the alley.

Brodie hesitated for another breath.

Tuck rolled his eyes to look at Brodie, his grip still strong on Darkly's throat.

"Now!" he shouted.

Thump finally came to his senses and charged at Tuck. His teeth were sharp and bared, flashing toward Tuck's last, lonely soul lights.

And Brodie? Brodie was done hesitating.

He jumped down from the dumpster and slammed into Thump before he got to Tuck. He buried his teeth in Thump's back and pinned him to the asphalt. He looked up into Tuck's eyes.

"Not without you," he said. And believe me, there was hard, unbending truth in his eyes when he said it. A truth that Tuck could feel, even more real and unshakable than the demon in his jaws.

Tuck blinked, once. Then he twisted his body ferociously, lifting Darkly's paws from the ground. He swung him by his neck and then let go, sending the soulless brute tumbling into the other hellhounds. The moment he let the demon go his feet were already running toward Brodie. Brodie gave one last growl to Thump and then released him and leapt away, running shoulder to shoulder with his friend.

"You shoulda ran," Tuck said.

Brodie looked at him.

"Go for a run without you, Tuck?" he asked. "Never."

Tuck flashed him a toothy grin.

But Brodie? Even at a run, even with hellhounds somewhere behind him, Brodie saw something in Tuck's eyes. Not something more. Something *less*. There was something less in Tuck's eyes, just like there was less shine circling his body. And what was missing from Tuck's eyes was . . . *Tuck*. Brodie could feel it, somehow. Believe me. There was less Tuck in Tuck now, and it made all of Brodie's heart and soul want to whine and growl at the same time.

His friend was fading.

Patsy was waiting for them on the sidewalk at the end of the alley. Brodie looked back over his shoulder before skidding to a stop beside her. Darkly and his gang were out of sight, still back in the shadows of the alley.

Patsy gave Tuck and his dwindling shine a long, unblinking look.

"What?" he asked.

"Nothing," she said after a moment. Her voice was quiet. She turned away, back toward the cars driving by on the main street. "Come on. Let's hop."

Their next ride was a red SUV with dark tinted windows. It slowed down when the car in front of it pulled over to park, and the three lost souls jumped inside just as it sped away.

"I don't see 'em," Brodie reported, looking back at the alley's dark entrance through the car's back window.

"They're not coming after us yet," Patsy said, licking at a paw.

"How do you know?"

Patsy glared at him, then looked out the window.

"Darkly just lost his last shine. It knocks you down, losing that last sparkle. Even if it wasn't his to begin with. He'll come after us, and harder than ever. But not for a while."

It was fully night outside now. The street was lit only by streetlights overhead and the headlights of passing cars.

"Great," Brodie said. "That'll give us a chance to get away. They didn't see which way we went. We'll be able to shake 'em now."

"No. We won't," said Tuck.

Brodie looked at him.

"Why?"

Tuck looked away. He was only dimly lit by the three soul lights he had left—one of his own, and two of Brodie's. They looked very small, and very fragile.

"Oh," Brodie said. "Of course."

Tuck had fought like a lion, and he'd taken Brodie's soul back from a blackhearted demon. But he'd paid for it with some of his own. They had his soul now, those hellhounds—or most of it, at least.

"*We* can't shake 'em," Tuck said. "But you can. They can't follow you now."

"No, Tuck. I'm not leaving you, I'm not . . ."

"Of course you are. Those dogs can follow me. In a little bit, once they start moving, I'll split off from you two. Take 'em in the other direction. Run till my shine runs out. And while I'm doing that, you'll be finding your boy. It's the way it's gotta be, buddy. Ain't no use fighting it."

"You can't, Tuck. You can't take that risk. What if you lose it all? What if . . ."

"It's what I want to do," Tuck interrupted. "I want you to help your boy. It's what I came here for. This is my second chance, Brodie, and I'm not gonna let anyone down this time."

"But, Tuck, I . . ."

"Oh, just let it go already," Patsy spat, her ear back and her eyes flashing at Brodie. "Why do you keep fighting when you know you've lost? He's right. And you know it. So leave him be."

Brodie's hackles rose. He wanted to growl, wanted to lift his lip and spit his anger at Patsy.

But Brodie? He didn't. Because she was right. He did know. He knew that everything that Tuck had said was true.

Brodie looked from Patsy to Tuck. He looked out at the night, speckled with falling snow.

He knew what he had to do.

"Okay," he said. He looked out the window. They were driving past a park, full of trees and bushes and even a big fountain, waterless in the winter cold.

"Are they following yet?" he asked.

Tuck closed his eyes, then opened them.

"No."

"Good. Come on."

Brodie jumped without waiting for an answer. He leapt far enough that he cleared the street and landed in the snow of the park.

A moment later, Tuck and Patsy flew through the side of the door, the cat dangling in Tuck's jaws. Tuck stumbled when he landed but caught himself, then set the cat down.

Brodie walked over to the cement fountain, which was dry and cracked, littered with papery black leaves. He looked up at the winter sky, which was crowded with gray clouds that blocked the light of the stars.

"What are we doing?" Tuck asked.

Brodie looked him in the eyes. He licked his lips.

"You sure about splitting up?" he asked.

Tuck swallowed.

"Yeah, buddy. We got to."

Brodie sighed.

"I know."

He looked again at the sky, then back to his friend.

"You ready to say good-bye, then?"

Tuck let out a low, sad whine.

"As ready as I'm gonna be, buddy." He looked around the park, and back toward the lights of the street. "Which way should I go?"

Brodie raised his eyes to the clouds. And just like that angel had told him they would, they parted for him.

"Up," he answered.

And then Brodie? Brodie howled up at that moon to call the angel down.

CHAPTER EIGHTEEN

There's something you should know about calling angels. It doesn't take long for them to show up. Because they're never that far away.

There was a moment, but only a moment, when Brodie thought it hadn't worked. The moon still shone between the parted clouds, the park still stood in winter darkness around them. A small tickle of panic fluttered inside Brodie.

But that angel? He came. Of course he did.

He didn't fly down on feathered wings, or slide down on a shimmering moonbeam. No. That's not how angels arrive. They don't really *arrive* at all. Because, of course, they're already there.

So when an angel answers your call, it's not like someone walking in the door. Do you know what it's like? Do you know that feeling when you first wake up . . . maybe in the morning, or maybe in the middle of the night, or maybe in the backseat of the car after a long drive . . . and you think you're alone, just for a few sleepy blinks, but then you realize that your mom is there, and she's looking at you, and she loves you, and you understand that you were never really alone at all? That's what it feels like.

The three friends were standing in the darkness by the empty fountain, and then they were standing in the darkness by the empty fountain with an angel sitting next to them. That's it.

"Hello, Brodie. Tuck. Patsy. Are you ready, then?"

The angel always asked. Even when he knew the answer.

Patsy's tail swished and her ear went back. But she didn't snarl or turn away. Angels aren't the sort of things you can just turn your back on, no matter how stubborn you are.

Tuck's tail went down. He looked at the angel for a long moment, and then turned to Brodie.

"That's it, then? You're just gonna give up?"

Brodie stepped closer to Tuck. So close their shoulders touched, and the glowing lights of their souls mingled.

"No," he answered. "I'm not giving up. I didn't call the angel for me, Tuck. I called him for you."

Tuck's fur rose and he took a step back.

"What do you mean? I can't go without you!"

"You have to. *For* me. Because, Tuck . . . if you stay here . . . if you stay for me and lose your soul and get stuck here, then I'm never leaving, either. If you don't go now, we'll both be stuck here forever."

Tuck's eyes searched Brodie's desperately.

"I can't, Brodie. I can't fail again. I can't fail you like I failed my girl."

Brodie growled.

"Failed? You didn't fail Emily. And you didn't fail me."

"But I ran away. I just ran, and I . . . I . . ."

"So what? You were a dog, and you wanted to run. You didn't leave her. You didn't fail her. You weren't a *bad* dog, Tuck. You were just a *dog*. A dog who loved to run. And then something terrible happened. That's all."

Brodie stepped forward again, closing the gap between them.

"And you know what? You never left me, Tuck. Never. Even when those hellhounds were all around us and they were taking your soul, you didn't leave me. You never ran."

Tuck's eyes shone bright in the moonlight.

"You did it, Tuck," Brodie said, his voice a happy whisper. "You did what you came here to do."

Tuck's tail started to wag.

"You think I'm a good dog now, buddy?"

"No, Tuck," Brodie answered, and for just a breath the words hung there between them, and Tuck's wag slowed to a stop. "I think you were *always* a good dog."

And that wag came back, strong.

The angel didn't say a word. He stood there and let those two friends talk, eye to eye and soul to soul.

Because that angel? Well, he knew. He knew that sometimes just waiting and listening is the best kind of helping you can do.

But he also knew that time is a thing that moves. Even when we wish it didn't. And he knew there was still a lot that Brodie had to do. So the angel spoke. And when he spoke, he asked the same question again.

"So. Are you ready, then?"

Tuck looked from the angel to Brodie.

"I think I am," he said, but he said it to Brodie. "But I can't just leave you here, buddy. I can't just go without you."

"You aren't going without me, Tuck," Brodie told him. "You're just going before me. I'll be there soon."

Tuck blinked. He ducked his head, then looked back to his friend.

"Promise?"

It was a new word to Brodie, but he knew it the moment that Tuck said it. He knew it, and he liked it. All dogs love promises, once they understand them. Brodie wagged his tail.

"I promise."

And when Brodie said that, he meant it. It wasn't a lie.

But it wasn't exactly the truth, either. Because promises are funny things. They stay the same, even when everything around them changes. And when that happens, sometimes they get forgotten. And a forgotten promise isn't exactly the same thing as a broken promise.

Except that, really, it is.

But that didn't matter right then. All that mattered then was that when Brodie promised Tuck that he'd see him again, he meant it. He did.

"Go on, Tuck."

"I'll wait for you, Brodie," Tuck said, backing up toward the waiting angel. "I'll wait for you there. In the long grass by the river. And then we can go to Forever together."

"Okay."

Tuck circled the angel, his tail as full of wag as a tail can be. He was Tuck again, his soul brilliant and undimmed.

The angel scratched Tuck's ears, he ruffled his fur, he patted his back.

Then Tuck stopped his dancing, but not his wide-mouthed smiling.

"Oh, hey," he said, suddenly turning back to Brodie. "You never told me what your *most* favorite thing is, Brodie. What is it?"

Brodie looked away for a moment, into the darkness, then back to his friend.

"I'll tell you later, buddy," he said.

Tuck's tail wagged even harder.

"All right. I'm outta here. Hey, Patsy!" he hollered to the cat still sulking in the shadows. "You should come, too! Don't you think?"

Patsy looked away.

"No," she answered, her voice final and cold. "I don't think."

Tuck's wag didn't slow.

"Okay. Someday, though, right?"

Patsy didn't answer.

"Someday," Tuck said again. Then he looked up at the angel. "Now?" he asked.

"Yes, Tuck," the angel answered. "Now."

Tuck's wagging slowed. He sat down beside the angel. He looked up into the moonlight, pure white and waiting.

Because Tuck? That good dog was ready.

But then Patsy broke the moment.

"Hey, idiot!" she shouted.

Tuck turned his head to look at her. He turned it reluctantly, though. Even Patsy could see that.

Because Tuck? That good dog was ready.

"Yeah?" he asked.

Patsy looked at him for a moment. Her tail whipped from side to side like she was fighting something. Then she yawned and looked away.

"Nothing. Get out of this dump while you can."

Tuck's only answer was a few happy thumps of his tail on the ground. Then he turned his eyes back up to the moonlight.

Because Tuck? That good dog was ready.

And then it happened.

Brodie didn't look away. Even when he wanted to. Even when watching his friend leave made him so purely sad and so truly happy at the same time that he thought he was dying all over again, Brodie didn't look away.

The moonlight began to sparkle. It became a beam of glowing, pulling lights. Tuck's own soul swirled and shimmered and rose to meet it.

There was lifting. And wagging. And fading. And then leaving. Away.

And Tuck was gone.

And the park was dark.

And Brodie's head dropped.

And Patsy sat in silence and stillness.

And the angel, who had never left (and never would), spoke to Brodie.

"You should come, too," he said. "You should come while you can." And the angel? He meant it. He really did. Because the angel knew what was at stake. And Brodie really was such a good, good dog. And the angel knew exactly how it was probably gonna play out. But there is a limit to what even angels can do.

Brodie lifted his head and walked over to the angel. He'd seen the way the angel had rubbed and scratched Tuck. And Brodie, right then, just wanted to be touched. He was a soul and he was a fighter and he was a friend but he was also just a dog, and he wanted to be petted.

The angel scratched Brodie in all the ways and places that he liked to be scratched. And you know what? That angel enjoyed it as much as Brodie did. He did.

"Are you ready?" the angel asked for the third time, even though he knew the answer.

"I can't go," Brodie said. "Not until I find him."

"I know."

"Will I find him?"

"I don't know, Brodie. There are lots of things I can see. But the future isn't one of them."

The angel's fingers rubbed into Brodie's muscles, scratched at his skin. It didn't matter that the angel didn't really have fingers, or that Brodie didn't really have muscles. It felt good, just the same.

"You don't have to do this, you know," the angel said, his head low, murmuring just into Brodie's ears. "The world goes on, with or without you. Your boy will have his life, with or without you. He has moved on. You should, too."

"Is he okay?"

"Your boy?"

"Yes. Is he okay? Can you promise me he's okay? Can you promise me he'll be okay?"

There was a shake to Brodie's voice. A shiver to his body.

The angel lowered his head farther, and pressed his lips to the top of Brodie's head. If he'd had eyes, he would have closed them.

"No. That's not how it works. I'm not allowed to make any promises, Brodie. But I can tell you this: Losing your soul to darkness won't make his road any lighter, whatever his road is. Come with me now, Brodie. Before it's too late."

Brodie pulled back. He shook free of the angel and stepped away.

"No," he said. "I'm going to find my boy. No matter what."

The angel stood. His face, if he'd had one, would have been almost mad.

Now, angels? They aren't supposed to get mad. But the angel was. Love can do that.

"You don't know what you're risking." He looked away in the way that only angels can, through the trees and down the streets and into an alley, and what the angel saw there was dark-eyed dogs rising up and sniffing the air.

"Those demons? They're coming, you know," he said.

"They're already on their way. And they'll find you. And there is nothing I'll be able to do to help you."

Brodie looked out, too. Out toward the humming darkness of the town beyond the park. A town full of houses and cars and light and shadows and demons and lost boys.

"Okay," Brodie said. "I guess I better get going, then."

And then the angel? He was gone. And the moon was covered in clouds.

Brodie almost choked for a moment on his sadness, and his loneliness, and his fear. But souls like his don't get dimmer because of sadness, or loneliness, or fear. They shine harder.

He looked at Patsy.

"You still with me?" he asked her.

The cat yawned, her eyes on the cloud-cloaked moon and her ear swiveling, following the sounds of the night.

"Why not?" she asked.

And then without another word they trotted away together into the night.

CHAPTER NINETEEN

The monster sat breathing in the darkness.

The couch creaked under him from time to time as he shifted or stretched.

The blue light of the TV flickered on his face, casting a head-shaped shadow on the wall behind him. The can of beer moved back and forth from his mouth to the coffee table at his knee. The TV was blaringly loud, filling the room with shouts and bangs and music and fake laughter.

Brodie sat watching him. As he looked at Aiden's dad, his fur never unbristled. His lip never unsnarled.

It didn't matter that Brodie knew that the monster could never hurt him again. It didn't matter that the monster couldn't even see him, let alone kick him or punch him. It didn't matter. The man on the couch still felt *dangerous*, still felt deadly, and he still shivered Brodie with fear. New words bloomed in his mind, and he knew them: *Sinister. Menacing. Evil.*

It was the last place that Brodie wanted to be. But it was the only place that he could go. His boy wasn't there, he knew. But there was nowhere else to look.

The room felt almost empty without Tuck by his side. Brodie tried not to think about Tuck. He was working hard to hold on to his hope, and thinking about Tuck being gone didn't help. He was glad that Tuck had gone, that he was safe and happy. He really was. But, truthfully? Brodie missed him. He really, really did.

Patsy sat beside him. Her soul lights swam around her. She'd lost one more on their car-hopping trip from the park back to the house, just in the running and the jumping and landing, even though Brodie had carried her in his teeth when he could. Just like Tuck had. She had only a small handful left now. Three or four lonely lights were all that remained of her soul. Brodie had caught her watching her lights from time to time as they had made their way through the town. She was quieter now. Her dark eyes almost never looked his way.

Brodie's lights were fewer now, too. He could tell. Not just by their lessened brightness . . . he could *feel* that he was fading. The angel had warned him. He could be lost. Forever.

And Brodie? He trembled when he thought about it. About losing his soul, about going dark and being lost forever. But Brodie sat there. He sat there and he kept his eyes on that monster. He knew he might lose his soul. But he was gonna lose it fighting for his boy.

The monster sniffed. He cleared his throat. Brodie looked at him closer.

The monster's eyes were red. Puffy. And they weren't looking at the TV. They were looking at his own hands. And his eyes were full. Full of things held back. Just like that girl's in the cafeteria. Patsy's girl.

Brodie cocked his head. He looked at those eyes, at what was inside them, and what was being held back. The monster, in that one lonely moment, didn't look so monstrous.

Darkness? It's a funny thing. Funny how it can twist, and tear, and torture. Funny how it can take a soul over. Funny how it *can't* take a soul over. Not all of it. Not all of it.

"So . . . how long do we wait?" Patsy asked, breaking the moment.

"I don't know, Patsy. As long as it takes, I guess."

"And what are we waiting for, again?"

And then, at that very moment, there was a knock at the door.

Loud. Sharp. The kind of knock that didn't want to wait.

The monster's head snapped up. He swallowed the beer in his mouth and put the can down. He shook his head, wiped at his eyes with a grubby hand.

Brodie rose to his feet, his eyes on the door.

"Who is it?" the monster hollered.

"Open up, sir." The voice that answered through the door was a serious one. Commanding.

The monster's eyes narrowed. He cleared his throat and stood up. Brodie followed him to the door, and peered around his legs as he opened it.

The front porch was crowded.

There were three people squeezed onto its cluttered darkness.

Two of them were wearing blue uniforms with lumpy belts and shiny badges. One man, one woman. *Police.* The word sprang into Brodie's understanding.

The other was a thin man wearing glasses, holding a box under one arm and some papers in his other hand. His eyes narrowed when he looked at Aiden's dad, and his mouth tightened to a line.

"Mr. Bondwick?" one of the officers asked.

"You bringing my boy back?" the monster asked. Brodie took a quick step forward and his tail went to wagging all on its own, but fell still at the officer's next words.

"No, sir. You know that. This is Mr. Loftus with Child Protective Services. We're just here for some of Aiden's things."

The monster bristled.

"You can't take nothing."

"We can, sir. We're just here for some clothes and his school things. You need to show us to his room. Now, sir."

That officer's voice didn't leave any room for argument. Even the monster could tell. And that monster? He was a lot less tough when he was facing someone his own size.

Aiden's dad sniffed and snorted, but he stepped back to let them in.

"Fine. It's back at the end of the hall."

They turned on lights as they went, flicking the switches and sending the shadows away. Brodie followed them back toward Aiden's room. His heart was a jumbled mess of confused anxiety. He knew most of the words that had been said, but he didn't understand their meaning.

One officer stood in the hall, his eyes on the monster.

The other one went into Aiden's room with the skinny man.

They started going through Aiden's dresser drawers,

taking out clothes and putting them in the box, talking to each other in low voices.

Brodie watched them, desperate to understand what was going on. He didn't like them doing this, didn't like them going through Aiden's stuff, being in his room. Aiden didn't let anyone in his room. Anyone except Brodie. He wanted to growl, wanted to bark, wanted to back them down with his teeth.

"I can't believe it," Patsy said, a step behind him.

"What?"

"This is it. You can actually find him. I didn't think you had a shot." Her voice was strange when she said that. Surprised, yeah. But not like it was a good surprise.

"What are you talking about?"

"Think about it, dummy. They're taking your kid's stuff. They gotta be taking it to him, right? All you gotta do is follow 'em, and there he'll be."

Brodie's head snapped to Patsy. Then back to the people, going through his boy's stuff. To the box full of his clothes. They'd found Aiden's backpack and put that in the box, too.

Brodie's tail found its wag.

"Yeah," he said, stepping toward the people, trying to look into their faces, trying to read them for clues. "Yeah. You're right, Patsy."

A pair of sneakers went into the box, a couple of pairs of socks. A jacket from his closet. The box was almost full. Brodie couldn't have stopped his wagging if he'd tried.

"That's it," the police officer said, looking around the room. "Let's get out of here."

Brodie scooted out of the way as the skinny man picked up the box and headed toward the door. But then the man stopped in the doorway.

"Wait. There's one thing he asked for." The man's eyes roamed the room. They stopped on the table beside Aiden's bed. He walked over and picked up the picture. The one of Aiden and Brodie.

"Yep," the man said. "Him and his dog. This is the one he wanted." His voice was quiet, his eyes on the picture. There was sadness in the lines of his face, in the whispery tiredness of his voice. Brodie liked him right then. He liked him a lot.

The man looked around at the messy room. It was full of clothes and books and old toys. A video game system sat on the floor, plugged into an old TV. He looked up at the police officer.

"All this stuff. And the only thing the boy asked for was this picture of him and his dog."

And Brodie? Brodie? Brodie's heart soared when that man said those words. But, believe me, *soared* doesn't cover it. Not even close. His heart glowed to a gold more glorious than any Forever. It shone brighter than all the blue skies and green fields and sunny days of anywhere and everywhere put together.

Because Brodie? He'd been walking in darkness too long. Hope had become a thing in the distance. And the sureness of love had almost—*almost*—begun to be replaced by the memory of love. And memory without sureness can pretty quickly turn into something terrible: doubt. And doubt? Doubt is no friend to a lost and wandering soul. Which was, of course, exactly what Brodie had been.

But then? But then that man said those words.

And all that darkness was gone.

And hope wrapped itself around him like sunlight.

And the sureness of love was like blood in his veins and beats in his heart.

His boy. His boy hadn't forgotten him. His boy, somewhere, was thinking of him. Waiting for him.

You. Me. Together. Always.

In death, just like in life, sometimes there is a reaching out: one soul stretching across the darkness toward another. It can be a scary feeling, if you're the one doing the reaching. A lonely feeling. But when, out of the blackness, you feel that other soul reaching out to you, too? Well. That is the best feeling. Believe me. At the end of it all, maybe, it is the only feeling.

And right then, Brodie could feel Aiden. He could feel him reaching out across the distance between them. Just like Brodie had been reaching for him.

Brodie followed the man and the police officers back down the hall.

The monster still waited in the living room, meanness and anger painted across his face.

"That's it, sir. We'll get out of your way now," the officer said.

"That's Aiden's stuff," the monster said, eyeing the box. "Be sure it gets to him. Don't lose it or mess with it or anything."

The officer blew out a tired breath.

"We won't, sir. We'll bring it all to Aiden."

The monster narrowed his eyes.

"Where is he?"

The officer's voice, when he answered, was tired.

"You know we can't tell you that. And I'd remind you that you are bound by a court-issued restraining order to not get within five hundred feet of your son. Aiden's temporary foster parents have a description of you and your vehicle, sir. You get within five hundred feet of them or Aiden, and you go back to jail."

"You got no right to take my son."

The officer, who had opened the door and was already stepping out onto the porch, stopped with a jerk.

He looked back at the monster. And, for a moment, there was almost as much anger on his face as on the monster's.

"You killed that boy's dog," he said. His voice was low and cold and quiet but terribly, terribly hard. "Kicked him to death right in front of him. And you broke his nose and blacked his eye. If the neighbors hadn't called us, who knows what would have happened. You don't have the right to call him your son. Sir. You're lucky the judge even let you out on bail. I wouldn't have."

The monster was seething. He was rocking on his feet and flexing his fingers. But even he knew better than to push it.

So all he said was, sulkily, "He's *my* boy."

The officer opened his mouth to say something more, his eyes flashing mad. But then he shut his mouth into a tight line and shook his head, one time, side to side. His eyes were as hard and sharp as bullets.

Because that officer? He was a good man. And he knew what the monster had done. And there were lots of things he wanted to say. But he was wearing a badge.

So all he said was this: "You stay away from that boy. Five hundred feet."

And then he stepped outside and closed the door.

Brodie and Patsy were left standing in the room with the monster.

Brodie knew he needed to follow the officers and the man with the box. He knew he needed to run through the door and hop into their car.

But he stood, looking at the monster. Words echoed in his head, haunting words about noses broken and eyes blacked . . . words he didn't want to hear, bruises he didn't want to see. The words made him want to run, run out the door and hop into the police car and get to his bruised boy's side as fast as he could.

But he didn't. He stood there, watching the monster.

Because Brodie? He'd spent years living with that monster. He'd learned to watch the monster's eyes and how he held his body and the way he clenched his jaw or tightened his fist. He'd learned how to tell the good days from the bad, the gentle moods from the dangerous. Before he'd known about words or angels or souls he'd known that monster.

And Brodie didn't like what he saw in the monster's eyes when that officer closed the door. He didn't like the way he tightened his fists and clenched his jaw.

"We going after them?" Patsy asked.

"Go," Brodie said, not taking his eyes off the monster. "Watch them. See which way they go."

"What do you mean? Don't you wanna—"

"Go, Patsy!"

Patsy looked at Brodie for a second, but he wasn't taking his eyes off Aiden's dad. She trotted out through the door.

The monster walked over to the front window. He pulled the curtain back, just a sliver, and peeked out. His jaw clenched. Unclenched. Clenched. He was breathing loud through his nose. He rubbed roughly at red-rimmed eyes.

Brodie heard car doors slam outside. An engine rumbled to life.

Brodie knew he had to run. He knew he couldn't let his chance at finding Aiden slip by.

From outside came the gravelly crunch of car tires pulling away.

Brodie was one breath away from bolting through the door and chasing the car.

But then? But then the monster muttered something under his breath. The words he spoke were only for his own ears. He didn't know there was the glowing ghost of a dog with raised fur and bared teeth right behind him, growling at his back. But there was. And Brodie heard the words, too.

They were: "I'm gonna get him. I'm gonna get my boy back."

And then the monster reached down to the couch and picked up his car keys.

CHAPTER TWENTY

The monster eased open the front door a crack and peered outside.

The police car had left. But its taillights still glowed red at the stop sign at the end of the street.

Patsy stood on the sidewalk, her tail swishing anxiously, her eyes on the car.

The monster stepped outside and closed the door behind him. He crept to the edge of the porch, staying in the shadows. His eyes were dull and glowering and locked on those taillights. The monster didn't know it, but a truehearted ghost dog followed at his heels.

When the car turned right and disappeared around the corner, the monster jolted into motion.

He lurched down the stairs, keys jangling in his hand. His car was parked against the curb—a car that Brodie remembered well. Rusty and run-down, with cardboard duct-taped over a missing window, and an engine that sputtered and coughed and dripped black oil like blood wherever it drove. The car door swung open with a creak and he heaved himself inside. Brodie followed him close, a growl in his throat and a snarl on his lips.

Brodie's heart was full, and not a good kind of full. It was full of fierceness and ferocity but also full of fear.

"What's going on?" Patsy asked. "Aren't we gonna follow them?"

"He's going after him," Brodie said. "He's going after my boy."

Patsy looked from the monster to Brodie.

"That ain't good," she said.

"No. It ain't."

The monster started the car. The engine revved ragged, but it ran. Through the window, Brodie saw him light a cigarette. Brodie hated cigarettes.

"What're you gonna do?" Patsy asked, looking down the street.

"Whatever I have to," Brodie answered. And then he hopped through the dented side of the car and into the backseat behind the monster.

The car was filthy, full of old fast-food wrappers and empty cans and rumpled-up clothes. It reeked of cigarette smoke.

Patsy flew through the door and joined him just as the monster hit the gas and the car roared away.

The monster was festering and furious. He muttered under his breath as he drove and his body was tight and jerky with anger. He puffed at his cigarette like a dragon.

But, like all of the scariest monsters, he wasn't dumb. He drove carefully. He eased the car up to the stop sign and crept to the intersection, just like he'd slipped out onto the porch. He leaned forward over the steering wheel, searching for the police car.

He must have seen it. Because he smiled. A hungry smile. A monster's smile. Fast and sour and then gone quick.

But he didn't move the car forward. No. He waited.

Because the monster? He was hunting. And hunting monsters don't want to be seen.

Finally the car jerked forward and they were off, driving under the streetlights.

"Listen, Brodie," Patsy said. There was an odd tension to her voice, a high pitch of energy. But Brodie? He was too focused on the monster and his broken boy to notice. "There's nothing you're gonna be able to do. You know that, right? Why don't you just hop out and howl and—"

That horrific shadowy memory flashed again in Brodie's mind: the fear, the danger . . . and then him running away, abandoning Aiden, and Aiden's terrified voice begging him to come back.

"Never." Brodie spat the word like a bark. "This monster attacked my boy, Patsy. He hurt him. Bad. And he's going after him again. I'm *never* leaving."

The monster was driving slow. They turned onto a different street, a busier one with more traffic. The monster kept his distance from the police car, far ahead of them in the night. Cars passed them as they drove. The monster barely blinked. The monster never took his eyes off the police car's taillights in the distance, and Brodie never took his eyes off the monster.

"This ain't your fight anymore, mutt. You're gone. Let them work it out. Get out for good while you can."

Brodie's eyes flashed hot over to Patsy.

"This *is* my fight, Patsy. But it's not yours. If you wanna leave, go for it. But Aiden will *always* be my fight."

You. Me. Together. Always.

Away. And Back.

Patsy seemed to think about it. She looked out the window at the passing darkness. She shifted on her feet. She looked at Brodie, then away, then back again.

And Patsy? She looked like she really wanted to stay. And she looked like she really wanted to go.

But Patsy? Patsy stayed. With doubt in her eyes and three meager soul lights circling her patchy fur, she stayed by Brodie in the monster's car.

There were more turns. More cars passed them. The monster was patient. He drove with terrifying focus. Outside, the snow began to fall harder. Big feathery flakes, falling white through the blackness. The snow hit the grimy windshield and melted. The monster turned on the windshield wipers and they swept back and forth, back and forth, streaking the melted snow into wet smears.

Patsy paced in the car, looking out at the night and the snow and the cars around them.

They took another turn, and the monster spat out a curse word.

Then he said, "Hilldale Heights? Of course."

Brodie stretched to see out the front window. They'd pulled onto a wide, three-lane bridge. At the far end, twinkling through the falling snow, were the lights of houses. A car passed them and zoomed ahead across the bridge.

"What's Hilldale Heights?" Brodie asked.

Patsy was circling even more anxiously now.

"It's a neighborhood. Other side of the river. Up on the hill overlooking town. Bigger houses. Your boy must be there." She was looking forward at the car that had just passed them, then back at the road behind them.

Suddenly, she stopped pacing.

"We need to get out," she said. "Now."

"What? Why? We'll lose him!"

"No. We'll find him—there's nothing else on the other side of the bridge but Hilldale Heights. But we gotta get out. Here. On this bridge." She crouched on the seat, ready to leap, and looked back over her shoulder at him. "Come on."

"Why, Patsy?"

"There's no time to explain. Trust me. Have I steered you wrong yet, mutt? Come on!"

She leapt. Her tail disappeared through the side of the door.

The car kept humming along.

Brodie looked at the door. He looked at the monster, still driving with his sinister stillness.

Brodie wanted to stay with that monster. He wanted to follow him straight to his boy.

But Brodie? Brodie had a good soul. Believe me. He did. And good souls want to trust. They do.

Even when they shouldn't.

Brodie took two running steps and jumped through the door.

He landed with running feet and kept his balance.

The monster's car rumbled away, spewing exhaust and dripping dirty oil. He watched the monster thunder off into the night toward his boy.

Patsy stood a ways back, under the glow of a streetlamp that rose up off the bridge's railing. She wasn't looking at him. The snow, so heavy a moment before, had stopped falling. There was only the starless dark of a clouded sky, and the yellow light of the streetlamp, and the grinding crunch of the car speeding away across the bridge.

Brodie trotted over to Patsy. She still wouldn't look at him.

"What's going on?" he asked.

"You trusted me," she said. Her voice was hollow. Empty.

"Yeah," he said. "So what are we—"

"You're an idiot," she interrupted, but there was no bite to her voice this time.

Behind him, Brodie heard a low growl.

He spun around.

Two hellhounds stood in the freshly fallen snow on the bridge. Thump. Skully. Their black eyes were steely and unblinking. Just like the monster's.

"Whoa," Brodie said, taking a step back. "Patsy. Run."

"Oh, she ain't running," a familiar voice said.

Brodie spun again.

It was Darkly. And Smoker. They were jogging up behind Patsy. Patsy, who still wouldn't look at Brodie. Patsy, who didn't even flinch as Darkly and Smoker trotted up and stood on either side of her.

"She's right where she wants to be," Darkly said. His gray tongue slopped at his gleaming teeth. His shoulders rippled with the ghosts of muscles. His eyes were all kinds of evil and hungry and triumphant. "And you, hotshot, are right where *we* want you to be."

CHAPTER TWENTY-ONE

"What's going on?" Brodie asked.

But Brodie? Brodie had a terrible idea that he knew exactly what was going on.

"What's going *on*, tough guy, is that you're about to lose your soul." Darkly stepped slowly forward as he spoke. "There's no getting away this time. Thanks to Patsy."

Brodie backed up as Darkly approached, but he knew there was nowhere to go. He was in the middle of the bridge with hellhounds at either end.

"Patsy?" He looked at the cat in disbelief.

Finally, Patsy met his eyes. But only for a moment. Then her eyes flickered away.

"I'm almost out of shine, mutt. What did you think I was gonna do? Just go dark again?" Patsy tried to spit the words. She did. She tried to make her words angry, tried to make her voice tough and hard. She did try.

But Patsy? She failed. Under that thin layer of anger, that painted-on toughness, her voice just sounded sad and sick.

Brodie took another step back, looking desperately around for an escape path that he knew wasn't there.

"What do you mean, go dark again? You've still got shine left, Patsy. It's not too late!"

"You think that's her shine?" Darkly scoffed. "Nah, she *took* it, just like we're gonna take yours. Ripped it off a little gray kitty she helped us corner. Cute little thing. Of course, that little kitty's gone dark now. Last I saw her she was trying to tear shine off of rats in the alleys downtown. Thanks to Patsy there."

"I didn't make her go dark," Patsy snarled, her tail swirling. "I took . . . just enough. She had plenty still when I walked away."

"Yeah. You walked away, all right, once you got yours. Didn't want to watch us finish what you started, huh? Thanks for serving her up, though. Just like this one."

Brodie suddenly spun and darted to the side, trying to get around the hellhounds behind him. They were ready, though, and cut him off with bared teeth and snapping jaws. Brodie backed up to the guardrail at the side of the bridge.

The circle of hellhounds tightened around him.

Patsy still stood where she had since the beginning, back under the streetlamp.

"How'd you follow me?" Brodie asked, stalling for time. "Tuck took back all my shine."

"We didn't need to follow *you*," Darkly said. "We followed the cat."

Realization washed over Brodie. The car-hopping, before the fight in the alley.

"You took some of hers. When you were all in that car together."

"Took? Hardly. She *gave* it to us, man, so we could follow you. Not too quick, are ya? She ain't with you, buddy.

She's with us. We take down the ghost, she gets her cut of the shine. Everybody wins. Except you, of course."

Brodie slashed his head from side to side, spinning and dancing to keep an eye on his attackers.

"I'm not going down without a fight," he warned.

Darkly bared his white teeth in a salivating smile.

"I'm counting on it. It's more fun that way. But you can't run. And we can't, you know, *die.* So the ending of this one's already written."

Well. There was a certain kind of sureness in Darkly's words. They felt true, there on that dark bridge. But endings are funny things. You never know how they're really gonna go, until they go. Just like beginnings. Believe me.

And Brodie? Brodie was a swirling storm of emotions. Panic that he was surrounded, with no way to escape. Fear of the hellhounds moving in around him ever closer, ever closer . . . and of that horrible feeling of his soul being ripped away. And a cold burning fury at Patsy and her betrayal.

But then, as he stood surrounded by evil, something happened.

New snow, icy and delicate as stars slipping from the sky, began to fall. Like it was blown from a mountaintop. Maybe by an angel. The snow began to fall all around them, as soft and quiet as the ash of feathers. But cleaner.

And for some reason, that hushed snow calmed and clarified the storm inside Brodie. Who knows why? But it did.

He raised his nose and looked up at the flakes fluttering down through the streetlights.

He didn't wag his tail. Because he didn't feel happy. He felt . . . sureness.

He looked back to Darkly's black, starving eyes.

"You can have my soul," he said.

Darkly's ears lowered. His evil wag slowed.

"What?"

"You can have my soul," Brodie said again. "All of it."

The hellhounds stopped their slow circling.

Patsy had been looking away the whole time the dogs had been closing in. But at Brodie's words, her eyes snapped back to him.

"What's your game?" Darkly snarled.

"No game. You can have it. You just have to let me go."

"What?"

"Let me go. To my boy. You can follow me. Let me go do what I came here to do. Please. And then I'll give you every last drop of my shine. I promise."

There was a long, tight moment of silence and falling snow and black eyes glistening.

Then Darkly's tail began its slow, sinister wag again.

And he spoke.

"The cat was right. You *are* an idiot. Let you go? Never. You're ours, mutt. Your boy is on his own." Darkly took another step closer. His black eyes were dull. Bottomless. His teeth were ready for the bite. His voice dropped low, to a scratchy rumble that was something between a whisper and a growl. "And what do you think you could do, anyway?

You couldn't help him when you were alive. You sure can't help him now. You're alone with your fate. And your boy is alone with his."

Those words. They jabbed at Brodie's heart with sharp little stabs. They shivered his soul with coldness.

But those words and that stabbing and that shivering did nothing to weaken Brodie's sureness. No. Believe me. They only made it stronger.

Because Brodie's heart? It would never retreat from the last ground it was standing on. And the last ground it was standing on was Aiden.

Aiden. His boy. The boy of wide-mouthed laughter, the boy of secret bedtime tears, the boy of fierce hugs and thrown balls and behind-the-ear scratches. The boy with the broken nose and the black eye who only wanted one thing: a picture of him and his dog.

I'll never let anyone hurt my boy. The words, the thought, the feeling of that pure unbreakable truth, ran through him like liquid iron; he felt his muscles tighten, his eyes narrow, his teeth shine, his claws flex, his whole hopeless self get ready to fight for his boy.

And that feeling? That feeling of desperate will, of full-souled determination to protect his boy? It wasn't a new feeling. It felt familiar. Brodie dropped his head, closed his eyes. And the memory, the full horrible memory, finally came back to him there on that dark bridge, surrounded by demons.

The mud. The fear. The anger.

The cursing, the thrown can.

Brave and beautiful Aiden, standing up to the monster. To protect Brodie.

Then the hit. Aiden crumpling. Brodie terrified, trembling. The monster looming, lumbering closer. His arm was raised, his hand tight in a mean fist.

And then: that feeling. The same one he'd just had, facing down Darkly.

I'll never let anyone hurt my boy.

And then: Brodie running.

Not away from Aiden. No.

Running toward the monster. Teeth bared. Heroic heart pure.

His teeth had sunk into the monster's leg before the monster's hand could come down.

The monster had roared and stumbled back.

Brodie had pressed forward, lips pulled back, ears tucked low.

The monster looked down at his ripped jeans for one ugly moment. Then his eyes slid with seething fury up to Brodie. And with a growl, the red-faced monster lunged.

Yes. The monster attacked. But with his boy at his back, Brodie had met him.

Aiden screamed. "Brodie! Brodie!"

Then it was a blur. There had been shouts from the monster, whines and growls and barks from Brodie, cries from the boy. There had been kicking feet and punching hands and snapping teeth.

But Aiden would not leave Brodie. And Brodie would not leave Aiden.

And then he'd been sent spinning and yelping. He crashed against the wall.

And Aiden had screamed.

And he lay there, hearing his boy crying. Unable to rise. Unable to help him. Unable to save him. And then the monster was standing over him, panting. He'd raised his heavy boot high.

Aiden cried out one last time.

"No! Please!"

And the boot had come crashing down.

And the memory ended.

He hadn't run away. He hadn't abandoned his boy. He'd fought for him. Of course he had. He'd fought for him, and he'd died for him.

And Brodie? He'd do it all again. A million times, forever.

Brodie raised his head.

He thought of Tuck. Brave Tuck. Tuck who fought. Tuck who battled. Tuck who never wavered.

And he thought of Aiden. And he remembered how his boy had fought for him, and stayed with him, and asked for pictures to remember him still. His boy.

And then Brodie said four words. He said them quiet. He said them to himself, partly. But he said them to Aiden, mostly. Wherever he was.

"You," he said. "Me. Together. Always."

Darkly heard the words. He didn't understand them. But there was no time for Darkly to wonder about them, if there was even any room left for wonder in that dog's dark heart. Because with the last word, with that whispered *always*, Brodie charged into battle.

CHAPTER TWENTY-TWO

Brodie didn't run at the closest hellhound. Or the smallest.

No.

Because Brodie was full of sureness. And full of anger. And he was full of Tuck.

And he was full of Aiden.

So Brodie? He readied his jaws and ran right at Darkly's waiting maw. He ran with his sure heart right at the beast himself.

Brodie's attack didn't take Darkly by surprise. Darkly had done this before; he knew that prey that is cornered will almost always, at the end, lash out. It's just how these things go. Almost nothing, in the end, wants to die. Believe me.

But . . . not being surprised is not the same thing as being ready.

Brodie leapt with all the speed that his spirit body could give. His soul sparkled as he flew at the dark beast.

Darkly stepped back; he swung his head and snapped with his jaws and swiped with his claws.

But Brodie's teeth found fur and held it.

Brodie whipped his neck, tearing at the monster.

Darkly snarled. Darkly howled. Finally, Darkly whimpered.

Brodie felt the other hounds close in around him. He felt their teeth on his back, his haunches, his shoulder, his neck. But he didn't let go. And then he felt it. The nothingness.

The nothingness of Darkly, the emptiness. The black blankness of a creature with no soul left. There was nothing for Brodie to take from him. Nothing more that Darkly could lose. All that Brodie could do to Darkly was to give him pain.

And Brodie? He didn't want to.

So Brodie let go. He gave Darkly one last tug and chew and then he spat him out and spun, all teeth and anger and sureness, shaking the hellhounds off his haunches. And then he stood, once again at their center.

Darkly had stumbled when Brodie had released him. He rose to his feet and took his place in the circle. His head was low, but not in defeat. It was low like a snake, ready to strike.

"Little puppy," he said, "is not playing nice."

Darkly's whiteless eyes had no sparkle, no soul, but they weren't empty. His eyes burned with dark hatred. And bottomless hunger.

Brodie looked into the eyes of the other hellhounds. He didn't see what he was hoping to see; there was no wariness now that they had seen his anger. There was no caution now that they had seen his fight.

Their eyes, like Darkly's, were brighter now. Shinier. Hungrier.

He had shown them his spirit. His hope. His heart. Brodie had shown them his *life*.

And it had made their lifeless mouths water.

They were starved for it.

"You ready, Patsy?" Darkly asked. "A deal's a deal. You get first take. We'll hold him down and you get yours."

There was no answer.

Darkly looked over his shoulder to where Patsy sat in the streetlight's glow. She was looking up, through the snow and into the darkness.

"Nah," she said after a moment. "I don't want none of this dog's soul." She stood up and gave Brodie one last, long look. "It's too bright for me." Then she turned and walked away through the falling snow, back the way they'd come.

"Suit yourself," Darkly said with a wagging tail. "More shine for us, then."

Darkly's head swung back to Brodie. His mouth opened in a toothy grin. And then the hellhounds swarmed.

Darkly surged forward and Brodie lunged to meet him . . . but before their jaws met, Brodie felt two sets of teeth sink into him from either side, one on his shoulder and the other lower, on his belly. The teeth sank deep and found pain there. Brodie twisted, howling and snapping at his attackers.

And that's when Darkly hit him. Brodie felt the collision, saw the blur of Darkly's yellow fur, and then felt himself driven into the asphalt. If he had been alive, with breathing lungs, it would have knocked the wind out of him.

Darkly stood over Brodie, his paws on his chest, and snapped quick and vicious at Brodie's neck. Brodie slashed his head from side to side, blocking Darkly's bites, panic rising in his throat. The other hounds were on him, too, nipping and tearing at his body. He felt fangs sink in, felt them hold, felt them chew and dig into him.

Then . . . the tearing. The pain rose, the agony. The ripping of his soul. One, then two, then three, four, five, six. Six pieces of his soul, torn away. Brodie felt each one as it left him, felt hope leave his heart in six painful pieces and felt despair seep in to take its place. Even as he fought and dodged and blocked Darkly's relentless teeth, Brodie could not stop the high whine that howled out of him into the night.

This would be how it ended. This was how Brodie would lose his soul, his life, his boy.

If he didn't break free, all would be lost. If Darkly got a grip on his throat, all would be lost.

Brodie focused all his energy, all that he had left, on one last effort.

He didn't jump up, or charge at Darkly, or try to lurch forward and shake the dogs loose.

Brodie gathered all his strength and *rolled*, hard and tight and fast, a wild twisting roll in the snow.

Darkly's paws slipped off his chest. One, then two, then three tearing mouths lost their grip. There were still growls all around Brodie, still paws and claws and struggling bodies, but when he felt the last mouth tear free he scrambled fast to his feet and spun, snapping and snarling.

Brodie was surrounded but he kept his paws moving, spinning and dancing and sidestepping, keeping each hungry mouth away as they came at him. He felt jaws close around his tail and he spun, shaking loose. He felt more teeth latch on to his shoulder and tore free with a snarling snap of his own. And he kept moving, kept fighting, kept his heart in his mouth and kept his teeth at the ready.

He was battling his way, step by tortured step, across the bridge. Toward his boy. With all those dogs around him and no place to run, no chance for escape, Brodie with his hero's heart kept fighting toward his boy.

Because Brodie? He had decided something on that snow-speckled darkness of the bridge: If he was going to lose his soul, he was going to lose it like this. Fighting.

It was hopeless. It was. Believe me. Brodie, that good dog, never had a chance.

Even as he fought, even as he bit and battled and bled for every inch he could make toward his boy, he was losing. One of the hellhounds would get a grip and tear with its terrible teeth for just long enough, before Brodie shook them free, to steal a bit of his shine. As he struggled and wrestled across that bridge, Brodie lost his soul one little light at a time. One to Darkly. Then one to Smoker. Then two to Thump. And another to Darkly.

Brodie was getting darker and darker and darker.

But there was no surrender in that dog. Right up until the end, right up until the very end, there was no surrender.

Finally, he found himself backed up against the concrete side of the bridge.

The hellhounds stood in a half circle around him.

Their eyes were still black. But around each of them were swirling bits of Brodie's soul. His shine.

They had more of it than he did now.

But shine? It's not the same as heart. They had more shimmer. But Brodie, even then at the end, still had more of everything that mattered.

The snow hadn't stopped. It fell all around them.

A car drove by, its headlights making the fluttering white flakes even brighter and whiter where they shone. Music from the car's radio could just be heard, seeping through the snow-wetted windows. It was soft, and sad. Something with violins. And a woman's voice, singing. The driver had no idea, I'm sure, of the drama happening on the bridge as they passed. A drama visible only to the dead. And to the angels.

"It's time," Darkly said. His voice was grim. Eager, but without the tail-wagging excitement he'd had earlier. Taking someone's soul for forever is a dark business, even to the darkest.

Brodie looked him in the eye.

"Will I still be able to help my boy? After, I mean? When I'm . . . like you?"

"No," Darkly answered, stepping closer. "But you were never going to be able to help him, anyway."

Another car passed. There was no music from that one.

Brodie looked at his shine out of the corners of his eyes.

Six. He had six lights left. He would lose them, he knew.

But Brodie? He didn't care about that. Not much, anyway.

"My boy," he said. He said it softly.

"Your boy," Darkly said, "has already forgotten you. I promise. They always do. Now you should forget about him. It makes it easier."

Brodie straightened his shoulders and turned his gaze back to the hellhounds.

"Never," he said.

"Always," Darkly answered.

But Darkly? He was wrong about that. The best hearts, the bravest souls, the strongest loves? They always remember. And they're always remembered. Believe me.

The hellhounds closed in.

"Only a few lights left," Darkly growled at them. "And I get the last one."

Another car was driving across the bridge behind them.

Brodie bared his teeth. He would lose, he knew. But he would lose fighting.

Just as the hellhounds leapt, just at that moment when their dark bodies launched at him, Brodie saw something. Just barely, just a flicker behind the beasts coming at him. Something flying through the air, sailing his way. A shadow, darting out from the passing car.

Then they were on him and he was fighting, slashing, to keep off their attack.

And in those first furious seconds, Brodie knew that he was done. They were too many, and he was too trapped.

But.

But then, in all the madness and the mayhem, Brodie heard something. A sound that didn't belong in a fight to the death between one good dog and four bad ones.

It was a howling, a screeching, a hissing and a snarling.

It was the battle cry of a cat.

CHAPTER TWENTY-THREE

The cat came out of nowhere. Well, she came flying out of a moving car.

But to Darkly and his hellhounds, it seemed like she came out of nowhere. It seemed like she had dropped straight from heaven.

She had not. Believe me.

But there she was, all claw and fang and fur and fire.

She leapt onto the back of Skully, just as the dog sank his teeth into Brodie's flank. Her claws dug deep. Her teeth sank in and found what they were looking for.

Skully's teeth let go of Brodie. He turned his head to the sky and howled in pain. And a soul light that had been Skully's for only a matter of moments floated over to the cat. And then the cat moved on, springing straight from Skully's back to Thump's.

Thump had been inches from grabbing hold of Brodie's throat when the cat grabbed hold of his. There was a whimper and a whine and a desperate pulling back. But it was too late. A light left the dog and joined the cat.

Darkly surged forward with all his ferocity and thunder but the cat was too quick, too ready, and Darkly's teeth snapped only at empty air and snowflakes while feline claws raked his snout and his eyes. Then a mouth, small but full of sharpness, found his shoulder and stayed long enough to pull one more light away.

The hellhounds pulled back, leaving Brodie with his back against the concrete once more.

But this time? This time, he wasn't alone.

"Change your mind, Patsy?" Darkly growled.

"Yeah," she replied, head low and ear back. She stood beside Brodie, her eyes on the hellhounds, and her tail swishing and whipping behind her.

"You came back for yours, huh? You want your piece? I get the last sparkle, but you have first dibs on what's left before I get mine." Darkly's words were friendly, but his voice was not. His eyes were unblinking. The ghosts of his muscles were taut and ready. He knew better.

"Nah, mutt. I mean I *really* changed my mind. You ain't getting any more of this dog's shine . . . not firsts or lasts. Not as long as I'm around."

"Huh. Guess we'll just have to make you not around anymore, then."

Patsy just hissed and spat in reply.

Brodie looked down at her. Her spotted coat, even in death, was thin and patchy. Her missing ear was a gnarled scar. Her ribs showed through her fur. She'd had a tough life, he was sure. And an even tougher death.

He wanted to be mad at her. Furious, even. She'd betrayed him. She'd put him on this bridge, surrounded by these hellhounds, far from his boy.

But Brodie's heart? It knew a hero when it saw one. And Patsy was a hero there on that bridge, even if she'd never ever been one before. You don't have to have been a hero before to be one when you really need to. We can all be a hero anytime we decide to be. Believe me.

Because a hero? A hero isn't a person. A hero is a choice. And Patsy made one.

"I don't think we can win this one, Patsy," Brodie murmured down to his fierce companion.

"You think I don't know that?" she muttered back. She risked a quick glance at him, then shot her eyes back to their tormentors. "You know, you could just howl, you idiot."

"No," Brodie said, thinking of Aiden. "Never."

"Yeah. I figured."

Smoker and Thump spread out to either side, closing the circle around them and pulling it tighter. The hellhounds crouched low, ready to spring. The time was at hand.

"The snow's nice," Brodie whispered to Patsy, who'd stepped in closer so they were shoulder to shoulder. The flakes were huge now, giant heavy fluffs that fell so thick they almost blocked out the darkness. Almost. "Aiden and me always loved the snow. If this has to happen, I'm glad it's in the snow."

"I hate the snow," Patsy said. And then she yowled and jumped with claws slashing right at Darkly's snarling face.

Patsy was smaller than a dog. Weaker. Her teeth weren't as big, or her jaws as strong.

But Patsy? Patsy was worth three dogs in a fight.

Brodie didn't watch. He was busy with his own battles. But he heard it. He heard her rabid fighting. And he heard the hellhounds, too; he heard their whimpers and their howls and their frantic scrambling to shake loose of her.

She kept at least two dogs busy. She took some shine, she lost some shine. That cat fought like a lion; she fought like a demon. But what she really fought like? She fought like a lost soul, cast into darkness, trying to claw its way back to the light. She did.

And Brodie? He fought, too. Even harder than he had before, now that he had a friend to fight with. To fight *for*. They fought. They fought fierce. They fought ferocious. They fought together.

And they lost.

Bit by bit and bite by bite, being outnumbered took its toll. They began to lose more shine than they took back. They landed fewer bites themselves, but felt more and more teeth digging at their own souls, and holding on for longer.

The swarm moved as the battle raged, tumbling and stumbling its way down the bridge, closer to the end of it. But not close enough.

There was a pause. A break in the battle.

Brodie and Patsy stood tail to tail, facing the doom that surrounded them. The hellhounds paced, circling them, licking at their teeth and wagging their tails. Each demon sparkled with stolen shine now. Brodie's soul was spread between them.

A train whistle bellowed somewhere nearby, its call muffled by the snow.

The bridge quivered. The train was passing beneath them, under the bridge.

Brodie could feel what was left of his soul. He had four lights left. Four.

He glanced at Patsy. She only had one.

"Howl," she said.

"No," he answered.

"It's bad, idiot. It's the worst. There's no coming back from it. You'll be lost forever. Like me. Just howl."

"Not while there's hope, Patsy."

"There isn't any, idiot."

He knew she was right, of course. But knowing and believing are two very different things.

The train whistle blew again, right under them. The rattle and clatter of it rumbling down the tracks echoed in the night air.

Brodie's head, which had sunk low at the truth of Patsy's words, swung back up.

"Patsy," he said, his voice as low as he could make it.

"Yeah," she said, flexing her claws and lifting her lip at Darkly.

"Remember Tuck on the truck, when we first met?"

"It ain't the time to get sentimental, dog."

"No," Brodie said, more insistently. "Do you remember? Tuck, on the truck? Do you remember how you warned him?"

"Sure. So?"

"*Think*, Patsy."

The train howled once more. Like it was calling an angel. The whistle was more distant now, but the bridge still shook under their paws.

At the edge of his vision, Brodie saw Patsy's head snap toward him. She'd gotten it.

"I think our ride's here," he whispered.

Patsy pulled in against him. The hellhounds drew in closer.

"On the count of three," Brodie said.

"No time," Patsy hissed. "Go!"

The hellhounds surged in, teeth first.

Brodie and Patsy didn't run. They didn't fight. They didn't jump up into the falling snow.

Brodie and Patsy disappeared. *Down.*

As the hellhounds rushed in, Brodie and Patsy dropped down out of sight, through the bridge.

All that the hellhounds' snapping jaws and biting teeth found was each other.

CHAPTER TWENTY-FOUR

If they'd been alive, it would have hurt.

There was a strange moment of humming quiet as they passed through the concrete of the bridge, then a roaring when they dropped into the night beneath it, right above the thundering train. They landed together in a rattling train car. It was a roofless car, open to the night air and full to the top with a shuddering pile of dusty black coal. Brodie jumped to his feet the moment that he came to rest, his eyes on the bridge they'd just escaped from.

They were in the very last car. They'd barely made it.

The tracks behind them were empty. But as Brodie watched, a shadow plummeted from the bottom of the bridge. It was a dog-shaped shadow, lit dimly by a few circling soul lights. It landed roughly on the dark and trainless tracks, then jumped up and began running after them. Thump. He was certainly determined, that one. But after a few stubborn steps, as the train pulled farther and farther away through the snow, he stopped and just stared after them.

Up above, at the railing of the bridge, three dark heads appeared. Brodie recognized Darkly's shape, even at a distance, looking after them. He could feel the beast's anger, through all that distance and darkness and snow.

Brodie had escaped again. But this time, not before paying a steep price.

He looked at the lights swirling around him.

One. Two. Three. Four.

That was it. All that he had left of his soul.

He felt it. He felt their loss. He felt cold. Lonely. Numb, almost. More like a shadow and less like a dog. Less like a hero.

"It's over, isn't it?" He asked the question quietly. Softly.

But Patsy heard it.

"What do you mean, over?" She was lying near him, in the pile of coal. Her eyes blinked up at the snow falling around them as they rolled down the track. Her one remaining bit of sparkle glimmered feebly around her.

"I mean, all of it. Me and my boy. Trying to find him. Trying to save him. It's over."

"Why would it be over, mutt?" Her voice was flat, fightless. Its edge, its growling life, was gone.

He turned toward her.

"Look at me, Patsy. I'm almost all out of shine. I don't know where he is. Darkly's got my soul and can follow me again. And I'm heading in the wrong direction. It's over."

And, just like that, Patsy's anger was back. She rose up, her fur standing with her and her eyes flashing.

"No. You don't get to just give up, idiot. Not after all this. Not after making me think that—after making me believe that—" She snarled, trading teeth for the words she couldn't find. "It ain't over. See all those houses there, up this hill?" she asked, jerking her head toward the forested slope that rose from the railway embankment. "That's Hilldale Heights. These tracks curve right around it. You hop out, you climb up the hill, you start looking for the cop car or that beat-up wreck the jerk was in. It ain't that big a neighborhood."

"What about Darkly?"

"What about him? He's been after you since you came back and that ain't stopped you yet. And it's all a mess now, anyway. Yeah, he got some of your shine . . . but some of what he took from you, you just took from the others, and some of what he got is mine . . . your precious shine is spread thin and all mixed up. He might be able to feel you out eventually, but you got time. Especially when we split up. He might feel us out here, barely, but if we separate he'll have to pick one trail to try and follow. You got some time, dog. And you got shine, too. Enough to get to your boy, I bet."

Brodie's tail almost started to wag.

"Really? You think I can make it?"

"Yeah. But you better go. Time ain't on your side."

"But . . . what about you, Patsy?"

"What about me? I'll be fine. I always am, mutt."

Brodie looked at the cat. That hard-talking, tough-boned, nasty-souled, chewed-up feline with the growling heart and her one little soul light circling around her. The cat who had betrayed him and handed him to his enemies, then came back to save him. The cat who walked alone, always snarling at the dark world around her.

"Why did you help us, Patsy? Why did you help me and Tuck the whole time?"

Patsy's eyes were on the darkness rolling by. She couldn't look at Brodie's eyes, at his dwindling soul, when she gave him the truth.

"I wasn't helping *you*, idiot. I was helping *me*. I saw all your shine and I just *had* to have it. You don't know what it's like, that hunger. I knew if they tore into you, there'd be none left for me. I figured if I could play you along for a while, maybe split you up, I'd get a chance to rip some off ya. Then Darkly cornered me in that car, and I had to make a deal. So I did. We'd worked together before, Darkly and me. We both knew how it worked. I deliver the goods. I get my cut."

"So . . . all along, it was just about the shine?"

"It was always about the shine," Patsy answered. "Until it wasn't."

They rode in silence for a moment, the train shuddering and creaking beneath them.

Then Patsy spoke again, her voice so quiet, Brodie could barely hear it.

"I shoulda used my shine on that kid," she said.

"What kid?"

"The jerk in the cafeteria. The jerk who threw garbage at my girl. I shoulda used my shine to sink my claws into his leg. Make him bleed. What's a soul for if you don't use it?"

"I thought we couldn't touch the living."

"We can't. But still."

"Yeah," Brodie said. "You should've used your shine. But not for that kid. You should've used it for your girl. You should've used your shine to rub against her leg, one last time. You should've used your shine to let her know she wasn't alone. That's what a soul's for."

Patsy blinked at him, then looked away.

"What do you know?"

But Brodie? He knew a lot. He did. Believe me. He knew all the most important stuff.

"Why don't you call them, Patsy?"

"Call who?"

"You know. The angels."

"Angels? What, like that guy that took Tuck away? Nah, he ain't no angel. There ain't no such thing as angels, mutt. He's just a person. A *human*. Dead. Stuck, just like us. They help us—or think they do, anyway—and they hope that'll help them move on. But they're just lost souls, too."

Patsy? Well, in a lot of ways she was a dark and twisted soul, wandering and angry and senseless. But sometimes, she knew exactly what she was talking about. Believe me.

Brodie, though? Brodie, with his true soul, was a true friend. And he wasn't giving up.

"Well, whatever they are, then. You can call them, too, right? Like we can? Why don't you? Because, Patsy . . . what you're doing down here, stealing shine and running from Darkly . . . that isn't a life, Patsy. I don't know who you're here for. But you should move on."

Patsy stepped toward him, her teeth showing and her tail whipping angry.

"A life? A life? What do you know about a life, Brodie? You had your boy and your warm house and probably a bowl full of food put out for you every day. I didn't have none of that. I didn't have nobody looking out for me. I ran and I hid and starved and shivered and I did it all alone. I didn't come back for nobody, idiot. I came back for *me*.

"You know what humans say? They say that cats get nine lives. Idiots. Nine lives? I didn't even get one, Brodie. I didn't even get *one*. I ain't going nowhere. I ain't gonna agree to being dead when I never even really got to be alive. I didn't belong here. And I don't belong *there*. I had nothing, I got nothing, I ain't nothing. And that's what I'm gonna keep on being. On my terms."

Brodie looked at her. He looked at the fire in her eyes. And he saw something there he hadn't seen in her before. A heart. A broken one, maybe, but a heart nonetheless. A heart with life in it, even. And where there's a living heart, there's always hope. Believe me.

When he answered her, it wasn't with fire or teeth or growls. It was with a step forward and wide-open eyes looking right into hers.

"I don't know about your life, Patsy. All I know is what you've been to me. It wasn't nothing. You were *something* with me and Tuck. All three of us, we were something. Car-hopping, outrunning the hellhounds, finding my boy. You have friends, Patsy. And you *are* a friend, too. Not a perfect one. But you're a friend. And that ain't nothing. You can do what you want. But I'll tell you this: Wherever I end up, wherever that place is, I hope you're there. 'Cause if I belong there, you belong there." He looked into her green eyes that he could see now held plenty of anger, yeah, but not just anger. There was more there. There was. He lowered his head so they were eye to eye, heart to heart. "You're not nothing, Patsy. Not to me."

Patsy looked away, out at the trees blurring by. Out at the shadows and the snowfall.

"You're an idiot," she said.

"Yeah. Probably."

"Get going," she said, tilting her chin up at the houses glowing through the trees. "Get to your boy while you still can."

"Yeah. It's time. One last thing, though, Patsy. You're not moving on just yet, are you?"

She didn't look at him.

"I figured," he went on. "I hope you do, but if you're gonna stick around . . . I want you to take some of my shine."

Her eyes snapped to his.

"What do you mean? You ain't got any to give, fleabag."

"I do. I got four left. Take one, Patsy. Please." She looked away again, but Brodie persisted. "Come on. You're enough of a pain in the neck as just a ghost cat; I don't think the world could deal with you as a hellcat. Go on." Her ear was back. Her tail slashed through the air. She looked at the lights glowing around his body, then looked away. "Patsy. You're down to nothing. You'll probably lose what you got just jumping down off this train. Take it. I'm not leaving till you do."

She blinked. Her tail swirled.

"I'm not," he repeated. "Take it. So I can go. Hurry. *Please.*"

Patsy growled. She started to turn away, then stopped. She eyed his shine, then stepped toward him. She leaned in and pressed her muzzle to his neck. He felt her mouth open, felt her teeth press sharp against his throat.

"You sure about this, mutt?" she asked.

"Yeah, Patsy. Do it."

The train rumbled beneath them. The snow, white and perfect, fluttered down around them.

And then Patsy? She did it.

Brodie felt her teeth sink into him, felt the stinging agony of the bite, and he fought every instinct he had to twist away, to flinch, to snarl and fling her off. He stood there as her fangs dug deeper and deeper, as her head twisted in a chewing tear . . . and then he felt it. Felt the shine break free, felt the painful loss of light, felt it rip away from him, felt Patsy tear off a bite of his soul and add it to her own.

Brodie whimpered. He couldn't help it. He closed his eyes and whined as his soul got smaller and darker.

Patsy let go. She stepped back. She sat looking away from him.

"Go on," she said. "Get out of here."

Brodie shook himself, trying to throw off the pain of the soul loss and the emptied feeling it left behind. He stepped to the edge of the train car, put his front paws on the frosted metal rim, and looked down at the ground passing beneath him.

"Patsy?" he asked over his shoulder. "Why didn't you betray us earlier? Like at the dumpster? You know you could have just let me jump down to help Tuck."

Patsy's answer was quiet, almost lost in the jittering thunder of the train in the darkness.

"I thought . . . I thought he needed it."

"Who?"

"Tuck. I thought he needed . . . to save you. To . . . Forever, or whatever. I . . . didn't want to stop him from getting that."

Brodie looked at her for a moment; then his mouth broke into a grin and his tail began to wag.

"You *liked* him!"

"Shut up."

"You did!"

"Did not. I just wanted the moron to move on so I didn't have to listen to him anymore."

"Whatever. You totally liked him. You big softie."

Patsy looked at him. Brodie saw, just maybe, a bit of the old fire in her eyes.

"Look, mutt. I been alive, and I been dead. And in all that time I ain't never had nobody look out for me. Ain't never had nobody care about me. And it felt . . . it felt . . . ah, never mind. We're wasting time. Get outta here before I take the rest of your shine."

Brodie looked at Patsy, one last time.

"See ya later, Patsy."

She blinked and yawned.

"Probably not," she answered, then looked away again.

Brodie grinned at her sulking, angry profile, then leapt off the train onto the snowflaked ground.

And Brodie? He thought, just maybe, as he was flying down toward the earth, that he heard three words muttered behind him as he flew.

And maybe, they sounded a lot like "Good luck, idiot."

And Brodie? Well, he was right.

CHAPTER TWENTY-FIVE

The streets and the houses all looked the same to Brodie, dull and round under a blanket of snow. The world was quiet. The night was still. All those living people huddled in all those cozy houses under all that falling snow. It was peaceful.

But Brodie? Brodie wasn't peaceful.

Brodie was running. And he wasn't looking at cozy houses or falling snow.

As he ran, his head swiveled, looking in windows for the familiar silhouettes of the boy that he loved or the monster that hunted him. He looked in driveways and down side streets for a beat-up car that leaked oil and reeked of cigarette smoke.

Brodie's heroic heart strained and sang and snarled. It had fought through life and death and day and night and good and evil to find his boy, to save his boy, and time was running out. He'd spent his soul down to its last noble lights. He could feel them circling him, precious and small and dwindling. They would be gone, and then hope would be gone, and then *he* would be gone.

But they weren't gone yet. So neither was hope, and neither was he.

If he was fading to blackness he was doing it with his eyes wide open and full of light.

He ran through the streets, heart bursting and eyes searching and soul burning.

And Brodie? He found nothing.

Cars passed him, but they weren't the monster's.

Shadows moved behind drawn curtains, but they weren't Aiden's.

He eyed parked cars as he passed them, but they were cold and empty and covered in snow.

He was turning a corner, drumming his paws through the snow, when he felt the first soul light leave him. He'd spent it, jumping down from the train and sniffing at the cars and running through the gathering snow. He'd left no tracks in the snow, but he'd been touching the world all the same, and it had taken its toll.

There was a feeling of pinching loss. Of a lessening. A theft. A pain as one-third of who he was blinked out.

His paws stumbled. He kept his footing, but he faltered. His pace slowed. If he'd had lungs that breathed, he would have gasped and moaned.

He slowed to a stop.

He closed his eyes, then opened them again.

He was at a crossroads. Two roads, each lined with lit-up houses, receded away in four different directions.

The crossroads was at the top of a hill. Below, he could see the train tracks. Beyond that, the blackness of the river. He saw the bridge that crossed it, the bridge he had fought at, the bridge where Patsy had lost and then found herself. On the other side, the lights of the city sparkled. They sparkled like a million tiny souls.

It was beautiful.

It was, almost, like seeing the bigger truth. All those people, all those dogs and cats and birds and souls and lives and loves and problems and promises and dreams and despairs. All sparkling like a brilliant blanket of lights under a winter sky.

Brodie sat in the snow.

He looked up at the snow-pocked sky.

If there was a moon, it hid behind clouds.

He knew that if he howled, it would shine. And the angel who was not an angel would come for him. But he knew he wouldn't howl. The angel knew it, too. He did.

He looked around himself, at all the houses in all directions. Dozens of houses, in every direction. If he picked any direction except the exact right one, he would run out of soul before he ran out of road and his boy would be lost.

But there was no way of knowing. No way to tell which direction to go.

Brodie's shoulders sagged. His head drooped. The world was too heavy.

His eyes dropped hopelessly to the pure white snow of the street.

Except.

Except that it wasn't pure white.

Right there, right between his ghostly paws, there was something in the snow.

Something very dark and very small but very much *not* pure white snow.

It was black and dirty and dribbly.

It was oil.

A single drop of oil.

It had, Brodie somehow knew all in an instant, dripped from a car with a cardboard window and a monster behind the wheel.

Snow fell thick around them, burying all the world in quiet hiding whiteness. But somehow, as the flakes fell everywhere and on everything, none of them had fallen on that dirty black drop. The snow fell all around it, but it had not been hidden or lost or buried.

It was, just almost, a miracle.

Brodie rose to his feet. His eyes were sharp, his tail stiff and still. His eyes raced around the crossroads, flying over the snow, looking for and then finding what he needed: another inky drop of blackness on the snow, a few feet away. He paced eagerly forward, his eyes scanning again, and again he found another drop farther on.

It was a trail.

A trail to the monster.

A trail to his boy.

Brodie's two soul lights glowed brighter.

He set off at a sprint.

CHAPTER TWENTY-SIX

The black drops led him down one street, and then in a sharp turn onto another.

Brodie kept his head down, his eyes on the snow, not wanting to miss a drop, not wanting to lose the trail. He knew he didn't have enough soul to lose the trail and find it again. He had one chance.

The snow stopped falling as he ran, the flood of flakes dwindling down to nothing.

Now all the night was a waiting stillness.

It was shadows and silence.

It was a dog, searching. It was a boy, lost. It was an angel, who was not an angel, watching. It was a soul, undaunted, but fading.

And then, it was a monster.

The car was parked in darkness, far from the nearest streetlight, beneath the darker shadows of a snow-curtained tree.

The engine was off, the windows closed, the inside dark. Dark, that is, except for the single red glow of a cigarette.

Brodie stopped running, his hackles raised, his lip lifted, his teeth unsheathed.

He stepped forward, right up to the car, and looked through the grimy window to the man inside.

The monster sat, wreathed in smoke. He brought a bottle to his lips and gulped a drink. Even through the cold metal of the door, Brodie heard his sloppy swallow.

But Brodie didn't look at the cigarette or the bottle.

He watched the monster's eyes.

Because the monster's eyes? They never wavered. They didn't glance in the rearview mirror or wander around the night or close slowly into sleep. They glared almost without blinking at a house across the street.

Brodie followed the monster's gaze.

The house was white. It was two stories tall. It had a covered front porch, and a basketball hoop over the driveway. The sidewalk in front of it, and the little pathway to the front door, were neatly shoveled. The porch light was on, and light glowed from the windows downstairs. A string of Christmas lights, white and delicate, ran along the eaves and wrapped around the porch railing.

There was only one reason that the monster would be watching that house.

Brodie walked without thinking across the street. He walked down the sidewalk, then up the shoveled path toward the front door. Brodie, for the first time in a long time, forgot about the monster and his soul and Darkly and Patsy and even Tuck. Brodie's only thought was on the boy that he knew was inside the white house with the Christmas lights glittering like souls.

He walked up the porch steps. The wood didn't creak under the weight of his body, because he had no body, had no weight.

He passed without pausing through the front door.

Brodie found himself standing in an entryway. The floor was a dark, shiny wood. To his right, a man and a woman were watching the flickering light of a TV screen. They were sitting together on a couch, facing away so that all he could see was the backs of their heads. The man laughed at something on the TV. His laugh was light, soft. It was an easy sound.

In front of Brodie was a staircase, leading up.

Somehow, Brodie knew. He knew where to go.

He walked up the stairs. He didn't race, but his step was steady and sure. He was a soul with a purpose. He was a promise about to be kept.

Away. And Back.

At the top of the stairs was a hallway. In the hallway were three doors.

One was open, and through it he could see a lamplit room with a bookcase and a large bed, made and empty.

Another was open, too, and through it Brodie saw a sink and a mirror and the edge of a bathtub.

The third door was closed.

Brodie paused. But not with uncertainty. No. Just the opposite. He paused with *certainty*.

Finally, after miles and mayhem and doubt and despair, Brodie knew where to go.

He walked up to the third door. The closed one.

If he'd had breath in his body, he would have held it.

Brodie walked through the door.

The room on the other side was dark. There was a window, looking out on the street. There was a dresser, some shelves. Some pictures on the wall.

But who cares? Who cares about any of that?

Not Brodie.

Because in the room was a bed.

And in the bed was a boy.

In the bed was the boy whose smile held all the happiness the world could hope for.

In the bed was the boy whose arms hugged with a fierceness that could burn away all your shivers and your trembles.

In the bed was the boy who hid under picnic tables in the rain and told you it was all going to be okay.

In the bed was the boy who would share a thin blanket on a cold night and shiver to sleep together with you and give you only the very best of dreams.

In the bed was a boy who would blink away his own tears and kiss you on the nose because he knew that you couldn't stand to see him sad.

In the bed was the boy you would do anything anything *anything* for.

In the bed was a boy who fought monsters away to keep you safe.

In the bed was a boy you'd trade your soul for.

In the bed was Brodie's boy.

In the bed was Aiden.

Brodie stepped up to the bed.

Brodie didn't have eyes to cry. He didn't have a voice to sing. He didn't have feet to dance.

But Brodie's soul? Oh, Brodie's soul. It was a bright one. Believe me. If you'd been there when Brodie saw his boy again, you'd have had to look away, his soul burned so bright.

Aiden was asleep. His eyes were closed. His mouth, barely open. His chest rose and fell, rose and fell, rose and fell. He looked warm. He looked safe.

One arm was flung out from the blankets. It stretched across the pillow, where his hand lay open and limp. It was reaching toward a little table that sat beside the bed. On the table was a single picture. The picture was in a shabby fake-silver frame.

In the picture was a boy and a dog.

This boy. This dog.

In the picture was everything.

Every part of Brodie's heart broke. And every part of Brodie's heart rose up from ashes into song. Everything inside him fell apart just like it was supposed to, and then came back together exactly as it had always been meant to.

Words? There aren't any.

Go ahead. Find your soul's one true perfect love. Then die. And lose them forever. And then find them again.

Then you'll see. Then you'll know how Brodie felt, standing in the dark room, looking at that brave and beautiful boy.

I don't know what Brodie would have done next.

I don't know if he would have barked, or jumped into the bed, or just stood in the darkness, looking at his beautiful boy forever.

I don't know.

Because whatever Brodie would have done next was lost.

Stolen by a sound that killed the wag in his tail and closed his mouth tight shut and snapped his head back toward the window.

Because standing there by his sound-asleep boy, Brodie heard the ugly unmistakable sound of a car door slamming shut across the street.

CHAPTER TWENTY-SEVEN

In the bed lay a sleeping boy.

Downstairs, a laughing man and woman.

Outside, a monster was coming.

Brodie was the only one who knew.

And Brodie had no voice, no teeth, no fists.

He had two fragile soul lights, on their way to shadow.

But Brodie? He still had his heart. And it was a good heart to have. Believe me.

He ran to the window.

Yes. There was the monster, standing beside his car in the darkness. His bottle was gone. Even from that distance, Brodie could tell the shake was gone. The terrible cold calm was there.

The monster's teeth were sharpened. His claws were out. He stepped away from the car, out across the snow-shrouded street. Toward the white house with the Christmas lights.

Toward Aiden.

No, Brodie thought to himself. *Not again. Not ever.*

Brodie waited just long enough for one last look at his boy.

His boy, there sleeping and breathing and dreaming, his arm outstretched toward a picture of them both, smiling in sunshine.

One look. One look, after all that seeking and searching.

And then? Well, then Brodie ran. Away from his boy. Toward the monster.

Again.

He ran away from the bed and through the door and down the stairs.

He was on his way out, through the entry and out the door, when he pulled up short and stopped.

He, a bodiless ghost dog, could do nothing against the monster.

But on a couch in the next room were a man and a woman.

And in his memory were the words of a policeman: *Aiden's temporary foster parents have a description of you and your vehicle, sir. You get within five hundred feet of them or Aiden, and you go back to jail.*

He ran into the room with the TV, ran in barking and growling and hopping high on his paws.

The woman yawned. The man chuckled again, shaking his head at the TV. A crowd of people on the TV laughed along with him.

Brodie barked louder, fiercer, more desperately. His barks were high and ragged and urgent.

Listen! he shouted. *Listen! He's coming! He's right outside! Look!*

The man and the woman didn't look. They didn't do anything.

Brodie ran frantically to the window. He jumped his front paws up to the sill and stuck his head through the curtain and peered out into the darkness.

The monster was still coming. He was across the street

now, standing on the sidewalk, one house away. He took one last pull on his cigarette, burning the end to a bright red angry eye, and then flicked it away into a snowbank.

Brodie looked back at the couple on the couch. How could he get their attention? How could he make them look out the window?

The curtain fluttered in front of his eyes and he shook his head impatiently to see past it.

He froze.

The curtain.

Brodie glanced at his last two soul lights, but just for a moment.

Then he focused all his energy, all his power, all his *soul*, on making his teeth real. On giving his mouth bite. He opened his jaws. He surged one last push of concentration into making his teeth real, solid things, and then he bit down on the edge of the curtain. Just like Tuck biting a french fry.

He felt it. Felt the fabric between his teeth. Felt the weight of it, the texture. He could feel it in his mouth. Just like he was alive.

Brodie didn't wait to savor it. As soon as he felt the curtain tight in his grip, he yanked with all and everything that he had.

He felt the tug. The resistance. The tension. And then the breaking.

There was a rip and a snap and then the curtain was tumbling, along with its metal rod, down from above the window, clattering to the floor with a perfect, noisy crash.

The woman cried out. The man jumped up.

"What in the world?" he said. He was startled, breathing fast. Brodie danced before him, tail wagging.

"What happened?" the woman asked.

"I don't know. Must've been loose or something. That was so weird."

The man's breathing was calming. The woman's body relaxed.

A small smile came to the man's face.

"Man, that scared the *heck* out of me," he chuckled, shaking his head. He sat back down on the couch.

Brodie's mouth dropped open.

No! he shouted. *No!*

It hadn't worked. A whine, shrill and furious, seethed in his throat.

But. But then.

"Well?" the woman asked.

"Well, what?"

"You're not just gonna leave it like that, are you?"

"Oh. You want me to put it back up?"

The woman laughed and slapped him on the shoulder.

"Of course! My goodness, are you the laziest man alive?"

"All right, all right!" the man laughed, jumping to his feet. "Didn't seem like an emergency, but if the lady insists . . ."

Yes! Brodie thought. *It* is *an emergency! Look! Look!*

The man stooped to pick up the curtain, then stood with it in his hands.

Brodie watched his every move, wired tight with anticipation.

Outside! Look outside!

As the man's hands worked on sliding the curtain back onto the metal rod, his eyes strayed carelessly out the window.

He looked up the street, away from the monster.

He looked up at the sky.

"Looks like more snow," he said. "Probably have to shovel again in the morning."

Then. Then his eyes wandered the other way, down the street.

Brodie saw them squint. Focus. Sharpen.

He saw the small smile slip from the man's mouth.

"Honey?" he said. "They said Aiden's dad was tall, right? Big guy with a beard?"

"Yeah. Why?"

The man didn't answer. His eyes darted across the street, to the car parked in the shadows.

"What kind of car did they say he drove?"

"An old silver station wagon, I think. Missing a window?" Her voice was getting serious. She started to get up from the couch.

The man dropped the curtain to the floor.

"Call the police," he said, his voice tight.

"What? Is he . . . ?"

"Yes." The man strode out to the entryway. There was the click of the door being locked. The woman had already grabbed her phone from the couch and was tapping urgently on the screen.

Brodie had seen enough. They would do what they could do. Now he had to do what he could do.

The police would be on their way. But the monster was already here.

Brodie had to stop him.

CHAPTER TWENTY-EIGHT

The sidewalk had just a dusting of fresh snow on it. If Brodie'd had paws that were real, the snow wouldn't have come over their tops.

The clouds had cleared, and the brightness of the snow was almost blinding in the light from the moon.

The world was all black shadows and white moonlight. There was no color. Only darkness and light. And a monster walked through it.

His steps were slow. Careful. Patient.

Brodie stood at the end of the house's little walkway. The one that led up to the locked door that stood between the monster and the boy. He let the monster come toward him. He had only two soul lights left, and after the pulling of the curtain he knew he was already very close to losing one of them. He had very little left, and he had to spend it well.

When the monster was only a couple car lengths away, Brodie barked.

He knew it would do no good. He knew the monster wouldn't hear it.

But he barked. Because barking is what good dogs do when bad things threaten the ones they love.

So Brodie barked. And the monster kept coming.

Brodie stepped from paw to paw. He looked up and down the street and listened, hoping to hear a siren, hoping to see the approaching glow of headlights.

But there was silence. And darkness. And the monster came two steps closer.

Then he paused. He stood in the cold night air, looking up at the house.

Brodie, for one hopeful moment, thought that it might not happen. That the monster had changed his mind. That he would drive away and stay away forever and his boy would never cower in fear again.

But then he saw the look in the monster's eye. A look that Brodie knew too well. Ugly, cold, angry, determined. It was the look he had before he slammed a door. Or spat out an insult. Or slapped a boy.

It was the same look Darkly had in his eye just before he lunged for your throat.

The monster clenched his jaw and rubbed at his nose with a knuckle.

Then he reached behind himself with one hand. He pulled something out that had been tucked in his waistband. He held it at his side, loose and lethal.

The moonlight glinted off black metal.

Brodie didn't know exactly what it was. But he knew exactly what it could do. He'd seen the monster shoot it before. He'd gone with him and Aiden and watched the monster shoot cans and bottles off a fence. Its terrible thunder had made him shake.

Gun. The word rose into his mind like a black weed, full of thorns and poison.

From Brodie's heart, from his soul, from his belly, and from his throat rose a growl. It grew and rumbled and shook and snarled.

No, he thought, glaring the word into the monster's unseeing eyes, into his furrowed brow. *No. Not my boy.*

The monster couldn't hear the growl, of course.

He couldn't hear Brodie's anger. Couldn't hear his power. His determination.

And Brodie? He couldn't abide that. Could not allow the monster to not know that he had come back. That he, Brodie, the dog with the hero's heart, was still by his boy's side.

Away. And Back.

So as the monster began to walk forward, Brodie focused what was left of his soul. He focused it on his throat. He made his throat real.

He made it real, then he made it growl.

The sound rang out in the moonlight.

It shattered the stillness.

The fierce growl of a dog who loved his boy.

The monster's eyes widened. He looked around. He blinked. His walking stopped.

He blinked again and turned his head from side to side. Not believing.

But his ears told him the truth.

The growl didn't come from the shadows. It came from the empty, silver, snow-dusted sidewalk in front of him.

And he knew that growl. It was a growl he remembered.

He shook his head.

Brodie growled louder.

Away! he shouted in his silent spirit voice, and he didn't care that the monster couldn't hear it because he wasn't shouting it just for the monster but for the whole world and for anything that would ever try to hurt Aiden. *Away! He's mine and he's good and you'll never, ever hurt him.*

Brodie forgot his shine. He forgot about saving his lights. He forgot about saving his soul.

He growled with his real throat. And then he barked with his real throat. A bark that echoed out through the night, ringing down the street and through the darkness and the light and into the monster's ears and even into the monster's own broken soul.

The monster took a step back, then another. His eyes were wild. He raised the gun, pointed at the empty air in front of him, the empty air that growled and barked with the voice of a dog that he knew was dead.

Brodie barked again and growled louder and he stepped forward, pressing forward as the monster retreated.

And as Brodie stepped forward he kept his throat real, kept his growl solid and loud, but at the same time he split his soul and doubled his determination and he made his paws real. He made them real living paws with real living weight and real living claws so that as Brodie stepped forward toward the monster, a perfect trail of paw prints appeared on the sidewalk. Paw prints that moved forward as the monster stumbled back, paw prints that showed up clear and sharp in the moonlight, paw prints that stood with the furious growling between the monster and the boy.

My boy! You cannot touch him! He is the best thing in any world and I love him! Me! Him! Together! Always!

Brodie barked one last bark, one last loud and undaunted bark. It rang like courage. It rang like goodness. It rang like love. If you heard that bark, you understood it. Believe me.

The monster? The monster dropped his gun. Right there in the snow.

And the monster ran away. Across the street. Into his car. The engine was started and he was roaring away before he even had the door closed. And as he turned the corner at the end of the street, he pulled in front of the flashing lights of two police cruisers. They'd been called to the neighborhood, looking for an old silver station wagon. One of the police cruisers turned down the street, driving toward the white house with the Christmas lights that had placed the call.

But the other? It didn't turn. It followed the monster.

Brodie stood in the snow, in the night, in the world.

He had barked and growled like good dogs do to evil things. He had barked and growled and he had driven the monster away. Away from his boy. Away. And never Back.

He had done it.

He saved Aiden. He saved his boy.

He looked at his shine.

One light.

Fading. Already, it seemed, drifting away. Barely held to him at all.

Brodie's soul was spent.

But his boy was safe.

And he had just enough soul to see him. One last time.

CHAPTER TWENTY-NINE

Brodie walked through that locked front door. No door could hold him from his boy. Not now.

He walked up the stairs. He left no paw prints on the carpet.

He walked down the hallway. He walked past the woman, who stood outside the closed door, her cell phone in one hand, her eyes focused down the stairs on the locked front door. She looked scared. But she looked ready. Brodie liked that she was standing there. He liked that she stood outside his boy's door, waiting for the monster. But the monster wouldn't be coming. Brodie walked past her, and through the door, and into the room with his boy.

Aiden, that beautiful boy with the long dark eyelashes, was still asleep. He'd slept through the curtains falling, through the phone call, through the barking, through the silver station wagon racing away. The monster had not disturbed his dreaming.

Brodie walked over to the side of the bed where his boy was sleeping.

Brodie. Oh, Brodie.

His one soul light flickered and fluttered.

Brodie stood there in the dark room and he looked at his boy's sleeping face, his gentle breathing. Brodie stood there and he thought . . . oh, he thought so many things. And he felt so many things. And he remembered so many things.

More than he could ever say, no matter the words that he got. More than anyone could ever say. Believe me.

And those thoughts? And those feelings? And that remembering? Those are just for Brodie. They are just for him.

There was a moment, or a million moments, or a forever, or no time at all. It isn't always easy to tell. Believe me.

But some time passed, or no time passed, or all time passed. And then it was time. Time for the angel who wasn't really an angel to come. Time for him to come to Brodie's side.

So I did.

I wasn't there, and then I was.

Right by Brodie's side.

He felt me come. He looked up at me. His eyes, if he'd had any, would have been wet. So would've mine.

"He's perfect," Brodie said.

"Yeah," I answered. "I know."

"I didn't call you."

"I thought I heard you," I lied. "Outside. I thought I heard you howl."

"No. I barked. I barked. I didn't howl."

In the bed, Aiden sighed. A sleep sigh. Peaceful.

"It's time for you to go, Brodie."

"I don't want to."

"I know. But you don't have any time left."

"Can I stay a little longer?"

"No."

"Can I wake him up? Can I let him see me?"

"No. It doesn't work that way."

"Can't he just pet me? Can't he just see me and hug me and pet me one more time? Please? Please?"

Brodie looked up at me. His eyes held everything ever in them. Standing there in the silence, we weren't a dog and an angel who wasn't an angel. We were just two souls. Lost in a dark world.

"No. I can't do that, Brodie. I can't. But . . . look." I pointed. To the last lingering little glow that circled that dog. "You've got one light left, Brodie. You've got one left."

Brodie looked at me, questioning. And then Brodie understood.

His tail? It wagged. A slow wag. A small wag. A sad wag, maybe. But still a wag.

And Brodie, with his last soul light ready to blink out at any moment, crawled into bed with his boy.

And me? I put a hand on Brodie. Just a hand, soft so he wouldn't feel it. But still a touch. Just enough to hold him.

Brodie, that hero-hearted dog, crawled up into his boy's arms. He nuzzled his nose into the boy's neck.

Aiden shifted in his sleep. He sniffed. He turned, and his other hand slipped out from beneath the blanket. It held a tennis ball. Yellow and faded. With the cloth tearing off at one corner. Aiden held that ball in his sleep.

Away. And Back.

Brodie saw the ball.

"Oh, Aiden," he said, and he wormed in closer, tighter to his boy. And he whispered four words into that sleeping boy's ears. "You. Me. Together. Always."

And then Brodie focused what little soul he had left. He focused it on his tongue, and he licked softly, just one time, his boy's sleeping face.

Aiden sighed again. And he raised his arm. And Brodie focused his last drop of soul on his neck. And Aiden's arm wrapped around it. And squeezed. And held. Warm. And strong. The boy's arm around the dog's neck, cuddled close in a bed. The boy. And the dog. Together.

The boy? That sleeping boy said in his sleeping voice one word:

"Brodie?"

And Brodie's tail thumped against the blankets.

And the sleeping boy smiled.

But the sleeping boy didn't wake. He sighed. And he kept his sleeping arm around his best friend.

There was a Forever moment. A moment that would make anyone's heart bigger. Even an angel's.

Then Brodie spoke, and his voice was as quiet and soft and happy and sad as a voice could be. I knew that he was talking not to Aiden, but to me.

"Do you know what my favorite thing in the whole world is?"

"What?" I asked.

"This," he answered. "This right here."

And then, with his boy's arm warm around him, Brodie's last bit of shine flicked out. And his soul went dark.

There was an immediate feeling of such cold emptiness, such deep loss, that if Brodie'd had lungs, it would have taken his breath away. His whole self, down to his deepest innermost parts, was nothing but dark and hollow. Brodie understood then the hunger in Darkly's eyes. He understood, and forgave, Patsy's betrayal.

Because losing your soul? There is no loneliness and emptiness like that. None.

But, for at least right then, Brodie was not completely empty. For at least a moment, he was filled with the feel of his boy's arms, and the sound of his breath, and the taste of his tears, and the total fierceness of his love. He was not empty.

Brodie? He was *not* empty.

"I'm gone," he said.

"No," I said. "You're here."

"But . . . my shine. It's gone."

"Yes. But I've got you." I pressed harder with the hand that I'd held on him. "I held you before you left. But it's time to go now. To Forever."

"But I can't. I lost my soul."

"No, Brodie. That's not how it works. You gave your life for your boy. And then you gave your soul. And a soul given is *not* a soul lost." I leaned in closer, my mouth close to his ear. "Let me tell you a secret. You can't lose your soul. You can't. You only lose your soul one time, and you lose it the moment you're born. Then you spend the rest of your life finding it and getting it back. You didn't lose your soul here with your boy, Brodie. You found it. And those little lights, they're not your whole soul. They're just the part you can sometimes see. But you gave some of your soul to your boy, just now. It's not gone. He's got it. And you gave Patsy a piece. And you gave Tuck a piece, when you promised you'd see him again. Our souls don't just stay with us, Brodie. They live in the ones we love, too. And they live in the ones who love us."

Brodie's eyes were still closed. He was still living in that moment when his boy had hugged him and said his name. But he'd listened to every word I'd said.

"Is it true?" he asked. "Is it true what Patsy said?"

"About what?" I asked, even though I knew what he meant.

"That you're not an angel. That you're just a person, another lost soul, trying to find your way to Forever."

I looked away, for just a moment, but I kept my hand on him, I rubbed it up his back, I scratched with my fingers into his fur.

"Yeah," I answered. "It's true. I'm no angel, Brodie. I was a boy, once. A boy with a dog."

"What was your name?"

I waited before I answered. Waited because it had been so long since I'd said my name. Since I'd even thought of it. But then I said it.

"Mark," I said. "My name was Mark."

"Oh." Then Brodie opened his eyes. He looked up at me.

"Did this help?" he asked. "Helping me, I mean? Did it help you at all, help you find your own peace?"

I smiled down at the dog lying with his boy.

Here's what I don't get: how the world can be so dark when there are hearts as heroic and souls as bright as Brodie's in it.

But that's okay. Because, yeah, the world can be dark. But in the end, at the end of it all, we always win. Believe me.

"Yeah," I said. "I think it did help, Brodie. A lot." And I meant it. I *mean* it. That's the truth.

"So you're gonna go on to Forever yourself, then?"

I looked away. Far away. In every sense.

"Soon," I answered. "I'm ready now, thanks to you. But there's still a dog I have to wait for. So we can go together."

We sat for a moment, Brodie and me, quiet. A boy thinking of his dog and a dog thinking of his boy. Then my thoughts, my heart, my eyes came back to that moonlit room.

I kept my hand on Brodie, but I stood up.

"Time to go, Brodie."

"But . . . what about Aiden? Will he be okay?"

"I don't know, Brodie. I can't make those kinds of promises. But I can tell you that there will always be a part of him that's okay. The part of him that remembers you."

"But . . . his dad. The monster."

I moved my hand in slow circles on Brodie's back.

"His dad is going to jail. And while he's there, he'll lie awake every night thinking about the growling ghost of the dog that he murdered, standing between him and his boy. He doesn't have a hero's heart, Brodie. He has a coward's courage. That man is never gonna bother this boy again."

Brodie lay, looking up at his boy's face.

"Will I ever see him again?"

"Yes. Yes, Brodie. You'll see him again. I promise."

"I love him. I love him so much."

"I know."

"This . . . Forever. Is it far?"

I looked at Brodie, lying with his boy. Held tight by love.

"No. You're not far at all, Brodie. In fact, right now, you are *so* close to Forever. We don't even need to leave. We can just go deeper into right here, deeper into *this*, and we'll be there." I scratched with my fingers behind Brodie's ears. "You are a good dog, Brodie. Such a good dog."

"Will he ever forget me?"

I leaned down, close to that good, good dog and the boy who he loved. There was the faint shadow of a bruise on the boy's eye, but there was also the faint shadow of a smile on his sleeping lips. In the morning, I knew, the boy would have the dream of a memory. Or the memory of a dream. Of hugging his lost dog in the dark middle of the night. And it would feel so real that he would know, in his deepest most innermost parts, that it *was* real. And he would go outside. And he would find, on the sidewalk, paw prints in the snow.

Impossible paw prints that came from nowhere, and disappeared to nowhere. The boy would see those prints. And the boy would smile. He would smile through tears, maybe, but a smile through tears still counts as a smile. In fact, it counts as one even more.

"No. This boy will never forget you, Brodie," I whispered. "I promise. Even dying won't make him forget his dog. Believe me."

I stood up, keeping my hand on Brodie. I could feel him slipping. I couldn't hold him forever. It was time to go.

"Are you ready?" I asked.

"I'll never be ready," he answered.

"I know. Are you ready?"

"I'll never be ready."

"I know. Are you ready?"

"Yes."

And then we were gone.

EPILOGUE

"Man, I thought you'd *never* get here! I've been waiting forever, buddy!"

Tuck's tail was all wag. His eyes were all shine. He danced around his friend.

Brodie wagged back. He smiled his doggy smile at Tuck.

"Did you . . . did you . . . ?" Tuck tried to ask.

"I did," Brodie laughed.

"And was he . . . was he . . . ?"

"He was, Tuck. He *is*."

Tuck danced. He ran three circles around Brodie. He leapt in the air.

"I knew you'd find him, buddy! I knew you would!"

Suddenly, he stopped running. He stood, almost still. His eyes looked into Brodie's, serious and questioning.

"So . . . does this mean you're ready?"

Brodie looked away. He looked at the dogs running through the grass, the dogs splashing through the water. The blue sky. He thought of that last moment, lying with his boy. He thought of the promises that the angel who wasn't really an angel had made him. Then he looked back to Tuck.

"Yeah. I'm ready. You?"

Tuck's tail went back to wagging.

"You know what? I am. I actually am. I was just waiting for you, buddy."

So those two dogs, those two solid souls, sat side by side right there in the grass. Shoulder to shoulder. They looked up into the sky, and beyond it. Both their tails were wagging.

"Are you afraid, Tuck?"

"Not even a little bit. You?"

"Nope."

Above them, there was a glowing. A golden beam of light stretched toward them. A glittering path of lights sparkled. Far away at first, then coming closer.

Brodie shook. But not with fear.

There was a tingling as the lights reached them, a warming and a humming.

"What do you think it'll be like, Brodie?" Tuck asked. "What do you think it'll be like, there?"

"I think it'll be like running, buddy," Brodie answered. "Only even better."

Tuck looked at Brodie and flashed his wide-mouthed, floppy-eared grin.

"You think Patsy will be there?"

Brodie's tail slapped at the grass.

"Yeah, Tuck. Eventually. Yeah, I do."

"Oh. Shoot," Tuck said, but he was still grinning and wagging. "Maybe I don't wanna go after all, then."

And then the light was all around them. There was no more time for words. There was no more need for words. Believe me.

There was a silence.
There was a song.
There was a rising.
And there was a moving Away.
And a coming Back.

ABOUT THE AUTHOR

DAN GEMEINHART is the author of several acclaimed books for young readers. His first novel, *The Honest Truth*, was a *New York Times* Editors' Choice selection and an Indie Next List selection. *Some Kind of Courage* was a finalist for the Texas Bluebonnet Award, and *Scar Island* was an Amazon.com Best Book of the Month. A former teacher-librarian, he lives with his wife and three daughters in Washington State. Visit him at www.dangemeinhart.com.

LIFE-DEFINING, DEATH-DEFYING ADVENTURES FROM MASTER STORYTELLER DAN GEMEINHART!

★ "A gripping page-turner."
—*Publishers Weekly*, starred review

★ "Exhilarating and enthralling."
—*Booklist*, starred review

★ "Compelling."
—*Kirkus Reviews*, starred review

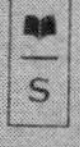